MEN

of OAK

Timothy W. Bryant

TATE PUBLISHING
AND ENTERPRISES, LLC

Published by Tate Publishing & Enterprises, LLC
127 E. Trade Center Terrace | Mustang, Oklahoma 73064 USA
1.888.361.9473 | www.tatepublishing.com

Tate Publishing is committed to excellence in the publishing industry. The company reflects the philosophy established by the founders, based on Psalm 68:11,
"The Lord gave the word and great was the company of those who published it."

Published in the United States of America

ISBN: 978-1-63063-838-2
1. Fiction Western
2. Fiction Romance Western
14.02.17

Chapter 1

Years of swinging the axe had developed muscles in my hands and shoulders. Dad had always told me good hard work along with time in the Book made a man strong in body and spirit. Swing after swing of the double-blade axe now brought this giant red oak that much closer to becoming firewood, lumber for my cabin, and garden mulch. "Waste not, want not" was Mother's favorite saying.

At the height of my next swing of the axe, a shot echoed, and a bullet snapped the head off the axe. The moment the oak began to fall in the direction of the shot, another shot rang out, and then I felt a burning in my side. I caught a movement in the corner of my eye just as another shot came from behind me. I barely had time to think that Thomas must be back there as I turned toward the movement to watch a man throw his rifle down, grasp his chest, and hit the ground.

The giant oak fell with a crashing, limb-breaking, ground-shaking thunder mixed with the screams of a man. I ran toward the top of the fallen tree still grasping the broken axe handle. Beneath the limbs of the oak, lay a man clearly dead perhaps from the crash of the tree.

Thomas, suddenly at my side, handed me my gun belt. I dropped the broken axe handle to buckle on my gun as we both turned to look at another man lying maybe twenty yards to the right of the top of the fallen tree. He was clearly dead, a gaping wound in the center of his chest.

"Who are they?" Thomas asked in a puzzled voice. "I've never seen them before."

We both had seen way too much death in our few years. I had met

Thomas during the Civil War he saved my life at Gettysburg. During that battle, a cannon ball had landed in the midst of a group of us; at some point, I had been knocked down and out only to waken staring at the business end of a bayonet on the end of a rifle. A body suddenly sailed across my sight, taking the soldier, rifle, and bayonet out of my line of vision. I heard a scuffling sound, then quiet. Then a stranger was standing over me offering me a hand up.

"I would have shot him," Thomas said, "but I was out of bullets, so I jumped him."

After that day, we were just always going the same direction. Even today he says I saved his life more times than he saved mine. Anyway, when the war ended, I had asked Thomas to come to Arkansas with me to build a home on land my family owned.

Yes, we know death, but death is something a man never gets used to. Who were these men; why were they trying to kill me?

"I suppose we should get the buckboard, load these men up, and take them to Sheriff Matthew..." turning toward me, Thomas shouted, "William! Will! You have been shot!"

*   *   *   *

I was having this somewhat strange feeling as if I had just woken up but continued to lie there almost awake but still sort of in a dream thinking, "Where am I, what day is it?" Then I heard voices talking about me, as I slipped back into the dream of a wild ride lying on my back in a buckboard. I could hear Thomas shouting at Red and Blaze, our two horses we had brought back from the war. Then darkness and the voice of my mother calling, "William, William come home; supper is ready." The darkness began to clear, and Dad was standing in front of me handing me a double blade axe; he had another axe in his hand. "Will, we need to get started early clearing this timber; we need the firewood, so your mother can keep that cook stove of hers going; a growing boy like you never seems to have enough to eat.

I know," I replied, "mother says it's

a full time job keeping me fed. Dad, you know I think she enjoys feeding me. She always smiles when I ask for seconds." More darkness, more voices- then I distinctly smelled coffee.

*   *   *   *

"Well, Doc, how is he today?"

"Sheriff, a normal man would be dead."

"Nothing normal about Will is there, Doc?"

"Strongest man I ever knew except maybe his dad or his granddad; I tell ya, Doc, this family grows 'em strong. I asked Will's grandma, Mary, about the strong men in her family. She said hard work and clean living make a man strong, body and spirit. William was ten when she died, but in those ten years, she taught William much of what she knew about living life and being strong. I miss her Doc; she and my wife May grew up together; our families moved from the east to first settle Hardwood."

"Hey, how about some coffee? I can't sleep forever! I got things to do!"

"William, don't try to get up! Doc, help me hold him down! "Will, William, you will open the wound; tell him, Doc."

"Listen to me, Will; Sheriff Matthew is right. That bullet tore a lot of muscle around your ribs and came close to your heart. If you don't take it easy for a spell, the wound will never heal right. The bullet ripped through your left side and busted a couple of ribs. Lucky for you, the bullet went clean through.

Now, William, quit trying to get up. I brought you into this world, so listen to me, and you will be okay. Sheriff Matthew and Thomas are here to help you. And Elizabeth is going to bring your meals to you."

"Doctor Michael?"

"Yes, Will?"

"If I promise not to get up, can you make Sheriff Matthew get off me, and can I just have a cup of coffee? It seems as if I have been smelling coffee for days."

"Let him go, Matthew."

"Ok, Doc; I'm not sure I could have held him down anyway if he had really wanted to get up. Will, I just made a fresh pot of coffee; I'll get you a cup.

You have been smelling coffee for days, three days to be exact. That's how long you been out, since Thomas brought you in. Here have some fresh coffee."

"Sheriff Matthew?"

"Yes, Will?"

"Who is Elizabeth?

"That's right; you have not met her. Well, Elizabeth and her family moved to town a few months ago and opened a restaurant. You really should get to town more, Will. She is someone you will want to meet; trust me, you will want to meet her."

I have drunk coffee since I was very young; come to think of it, I do not really remember ever not drinking coffee. However, this cup-its taste and smell- may be the best, the very best cup I have ever had. Why is it so good? Has Sheriff Matthew started using a different brand of coffee? Is there a different brand of coffee? I see the same old blue and white speckled metal coffee pot setting on that same potbelly wood stove, the same pot that I have drunk many a cup of coffee from. This cup felt so good goin' down. As I swallow, even the grounds that I always remember seem to be in Sheriff Matthew's coffee, taste good going down. Maybe it has something to do with my being out for three days. Why is it so important to Sheriff Matthew, my friend, that I meet Elizabeth?

I finished the coffee and really wanted another, but my eyes were suddenly heavy. Well, the next time I woke to the smell of food, and the sounds of Sheriff Matthew and the Doc engaged in a conversation with a young lady.

As I opened my eyes, she was moving about the room giving the Sheriff a hard time as to how dirty his office and my jail cell were. She was saying something about men not really understanding the meaning of clean. She noticed almost immediately when I opened my eyes; she came straight to me, leaned over me, and said, "Hey."

My mother always seemed to be one of the most beautiful women I knew, but that just changed, only different somehow. As she leaned over me, her long brown hair fell off her shoulders and her dark brown eyes looked into mine. "William O'Brien, you are alive."

"Will, this is Elizabeth Lane." Now Sheriff Matthew was leaning over me, grinning like a possum.

"Sheriff, did Thomas leave me my gun belt?"

"Yes, he did, Will."

"Good; go get it for me, Sheriff."

"Why, Will?" he asked, still grinning like a possum.

"Because, I'm going to shoot you, Sheriff Matthew."

*   *   *   *

It had been a while so the axe felt good in my hand; the red oak wood was splitting easily. Maybe I should not be doing this yet, but a man can lie in bed only so long without going crazy. As I looked up Thomas came riding in on Red.

"Hey, Will, should you be up and splitting wood?"

"Depends on who you ask! If you ask any of my nurses, they would say no, but here I am splitting wood."

"William, you know they might be right; it has been only a week. I have seen one of your nurses, she's not so bad. In fact, those days you were out, the Lanes kept me fed. I tell you if Elizabeth can cook half as good as her mother Mary, well, I'll just say a man would be nuts not to want a woman like that around."

"Thanks, Thomas, but why are you telling me? I just met her, Elizabeth, that is."

"I am just saying, Will--"

"Ok, thanks again, Thomas; between you and the Sheriff, ya'll will have me married with five kids already."

"No, William, I didn't mean to—well, you will figure it out."

"Yep, I will, but beside that, thanks for bringing me to town. Sheriff Matthew said he thought you didn't sleep those three days I was out, and he said you and your gun never left my side."

"May be true, Will, but you would have done the same if it had been me instead."

Chapter 2

Walking across the street, I could see into the Lanes' restaurant; four steps led up to the glass front doors.

A large man had a woman by the arm, and as I watched, he roughly shoved her to the floor, still holding her arm. The four steps up into the restaurant became one-step, and I was inside, hearing this man saying loudly, "I am not waiting! Find me a place to sit and bring me some food, woman!"

With enough force to get his attention, I slapped the hat off his head. He released the woman and turned to face me. The woman was Elizabeth. There had been times during the war when in the heat of battle, a blood boiling fury had come over me, and I had became someone I was ashamed of later. Pastor Luke spent a lot of time around our fire helping me and Thomas come to grip with our past; he had also fought in the war. But, this was different; as this stranger turned, we were eye to eye. Grabbing his collar in one hand and his belt buckle in the other, I lifted him off his feet onto my shoulders. I turned to make my way through the front doors held open by two men as if they knew what I was going to do. With blood-boiling fury, I lifted him off my shoulders and standing on the walk threw him four steps down into the street.

In one movement, without thinking, I turned back inside to help Elizabeth up. She was already up and mad.

"Are you okay, Elizabeth?"

Her eyes suddenly open wider; then she screamed, "Will!"

I felt something hit the side of my head taking me to the floor. As I rolled over to look up at the big man I had just thrown into the street, Bud Tillman, his boot lifted to stomp my head in. Suddenly, his eyes rolled back in his head, and he fell on top of me. I could see Elizabeth standing over both of us still very mad and her dad, Charles Lane, taking the steel poker from her hands.

"Its okay, Elizabeth; he is down and out," Charles said quietly. "That will teach him to lay hold of a woman roughly.

"Oh William, are you all right?"

"I will be, Elizabeth, if someone can get Bud off me."

Sheriff Matthew and Thomas had been across the street when they saw me throwing Bud Tillman into the street. Well, they neither one thought this seemed normal, so both had run across the street in time to lift Bud off me. The Sheriff looked at me, Elizabeth, and the steel poker.

"Looks as if Bud was trying to bully the wrong two people", commented Sheriff Matthew.

"Is he dead, Sheriff?" Elizabeth asked.

"No, Elizabeth, but he is going to have a nasty headache." "Well, he should not have grabbed me. "William?" As she said my name, she drops to the floor beside me, placing her hand on my chest. "Are you okay? How did you do that?"

"He had a hold on you, Elizabeth; I couldn't allow that." She did not say anything, just looked at me with those brown eyes.

"You know, Will, normally when I sew a man up and treat him after a serious gunshot wound, I advise him not to be lifting large men over his head and throwing them into the street for at least six months."

"Well, Doc, it just seemed like the thing to do at the time. Now if I could get up off the floor I would love a cup of coffee and some breakfast."

As I came off the floor, I had an arm around Elizabeth or she had an arm around me, hard to tell which. When we were both standing, in each other's arms, we both looked around at everyone in the restaurant, all smiling and looking at us. Elizabeth released her hold on me, or maybe I released my hold on her.

"There is a table by the fire place; I'll bring you that coffee," she said softly.

As she took a step away, I touched her shoulder, turning her to look at me. "Thanks, Elizabeth."

Charles brought me coffee. "William, Mary and Elizabeth are fixin your breakfast, and thanks for helping our daughter. I put that bully out once myself when he got loud with Mary. She had gone after her frying pan, but I had my double barrel shotgun handy. I asked him to leave politely as I pointed it toward him and pulled both hammers back. God help me, I would have shot him without hesitation after the way he talked to Mary. I do not care how big and strong a man is; a double barrel shotgun loaded with buckshot will kill him, and now, after the way he laid hold on Elizabeth-- mind if I sit with you, William?"

"Course not, Mr. Lane, it's your restaurant."

"Call me Charles, William."

"Thanks you, Charles."

"Before I married Mary and once little Elizabeth came along, I was a man given to trouble not always looking for it but never one to find a way to avoid it. Most of my past trouble was because of the gun I wore. After I met, Mary her dad taught me his trade; butchering, smoking, and curing meat. Then one day, I just didn't put my gun on, but I will put my gun back on to keep harm from Mary and Elizabeth."

"If it comes to that, Charles, I will be at your side."

"Thanks William, that's good to know."

"Call me Will, Charles; all my friends do."

The doors to the kitchen came open, and a woman carried two plates of great smelling food and placed them on the table in front of me. I stood up because a woman had entered the room; my momma taught me stand up when a woman enters the room. This woman grabbed me in a big hug; she was very strong.

"William, this is my wife Mary."

*　　*　　*　　*

"Now, Bud you listen to me; stay clear of town. You are lucky Sheriff Matthew did not keep you in jail any longer than it took the Doc to patch up your head. Did I hear a woman did that to you?"

"Mister Rocman, Sheriff Matthew had no right to talk to me the way he did, and as for that woman, there will be another time."

"You are not listening to me, Bud; stay away from those folks. If you don't, my plans will be ruined" Bud noticed and for some reason had never noticed before, standing face to face with Mister Rocman, Rocman was actually a few inches taller than he. That was something Bud was not used to, having always been taller and bigger; thus knowing, he was stronger than any other man he had ever met.

Come to think of it how did that man back at the restaurant pick me up and toss me into the street? That did not seem possible and where is my hat? Bud wondered almost as an afterthought.

Snapped back to present by

Rocmans" hand on his shoulder and feeling the grip, he wondered if there may be more to Rocman than that fancy jacket he always wore.

"Listen, Bud, I have a job for you, and it will keep you away from Hardwood for a while. Take this letter to Memphis."

"Wait a minute, Mister Rocman; Memphis? Are you crazy? I am not going to Memphis!"

"Oh yes, you are," with the grip getting somewhat tighter on my shoulder, "if you want to keep the money I have already given you plus much more and the land we will have, you will. There is more going on here than you know, Bud. I will do it with you or without you, your choice. If it is revenge you need, I saw that man toss you into the street. His name is William O'Brien."

Seeing the interest come over Bud's face Rocman continued, "My first attempt to be rid of Mister O'Brien failed, but there will be others. Now, back to this trip to Memphis; we need more men; the kinds of men we need are in the employment of a certain man,

Saul Rocman."

"He some kinfolk of yours, Mister Rocman?"

"Yes, if you need to know, he's my brother; our mother read us the Bible regularly and named us after kings. Our father did not read the Bible; most of what I know came from him.

Now listen, when you get back with these men. Take them down river from town about a mile. There is an old, rather large cabin; I have purchased one-hundred acres around the cabin. At one time there was a lead mine there, so we are going to start back up the mine."

"But Mister Rocman is there any money to be made in lead mining? I have heard there are old lead mines all around this part of the country."

"Yes, Bud, you're right, but we need some reason to be bringing these men here without arousing suspicions. Bud you ask too many questions. Here is a letter to my brother, and some money for the trip. Get going, the sooner you are gone the better since you have stirred up enough trouble already. I do not need any enemies yet, later, it will not matter."

"Yes, Mister Rocman you know this will take me a few weeks."

"Take a month, Bud; when you get to Memphis, my brother will have a place for you. I will use the time you are gone to establish myself as a respectable citizen in Hardwood.

Rocman watched thoughtfully as Bud slipped a foot into the stirrup and settled in the saddle, he felt sorry for the saddle and the horse, a large horse but still Bud was a big man.

Then an odd thought popped into his mind-- how did that man in town best him? His next thought disturbed him: "I need to meet this man; perhaps he can be of some help to me."

Chapter 3

"Mary, let the young man go so he can eat." chuckled Charles.

"Yes, William do sit down and eat. I just—well, Elizabeth has spoken of you so much since Sheriff Matthew introduced you two. Seeing you take care of that horrible man the way you did-- I never saw such strength in a man, yet when I look into your eyes, I see a man not wanting to hurt a living soul."

"Mary, come on; let the man eat. I think you may be embarrassing him."

"I am sorry, William; Elizabeth is bringing a fresh pot of coffee. I hope you like fresh, smoked bacon, biscuits, and sausage gravy. I brought you scrambled eggs and some fried potatoes. Also, some apple strawberry preserves and fresh- out-of-the-oven sourdough bread.

"Thanks, Mrs. Lane; this is quite enough. Will it upset you if I eat all of it? I just really got my appetite back."

"No, of course not, William, and call me Mary."

"Thanks Mary; you know my grandmother's name was Mary."

"Yes, I know, William; she is well spoken of in Hardwood, as is your grandfather, your dad, and your mother.

Just then Elizabeth came into the room real sudden like; my quickly standing up stopped her, as she began pouring, "Will, how do you like your coffee?"

"Black"

"Please sit, Will and finish your breakfast; Mom, you brought enough food out to feed five men."

"He looks hungry, Elizabeth." Mary observed as she turned, "Will, you are still standing and Elizabeth, you seem upset about something."

"I am; the fire in the stove had died down, and the water would not boil to make you a fresh pot of coffee."

"Elizabeth, I had just stoked the fire in that stove; it was almost glowing red. Could it be that you were in a hurry for the water to boil. Maybe so you could bring it out to someone?"

"I am sure I do not know what you are talking about! Will, why are you still standing?"

I reached beside where I had been sitting and pulled out a chair. "I would like to sit and finish my breakfast, if you would sit with me Elizabeth."

As she sat down beside me, all of a sudden Charles and Mary had work to do in the kitchen. Then Mary came back with an empty cup she sat down in front of Elizabeth. "Take your time eating, William; the breakfast rush is over. That whole pot of coffee is for you and Elizabeth. Here is cream for you, Elizabeth."

"Thanks, Mom."

"How 'bout you, William; do you need cream or sugar for your coffee?"

"No, mom; he drinks it black like

dad."

As I ate, Elizabeth sipped her coffee and nibbled a piece of bread with strawberry preserves. "You will want some of these preserves; made them myself from wild strawberries I found on the side of a hill just south of town overlooking the river."

"I know the spot; my mother and grandmother picked strawberries there for years."

"Does your family own that land?"

"No, our land runs north of the river. There was a man owned that land, and there was some lead mining done, but he never made a go of it. I heard he wanted to sell out; said he was moving to Memphis to work on the big riverboats. Nobody here had any money, so I guess he still owns it. That was a few years before the war."

"Will, did you know we met your granddad and he is the main reason we moved here?"

How? Where? Is he alive?"

"We met in Gettysburg during the war, but before the big battle there. He ate in our restaurant many times; Dad and he became good friends. He told us he had a grandson, and when I first saw you, I knew you were kin-very strong family resemblance. He might be a little taller than you, maybe not."

"No, he is not taller than me, at least not the last time we measured back to back. It was a thing between us; Mother said we were going to strain something, both stretching to be taller than the other. Mother and Dad were always the judges to say who was taller. Last time Mother said I was taller, with Dad saying it could go either way."

"Will, what of your Mother and Dad?"

"It is hard to talk about."

"Sorry, Will, I don't mean to pry."

"No, I should talk about it. When the war broke out, I was about seventeen and felt a strong need to be in the middle of it. Looking back, I recognize my justification was that I hated slavery and had been brought up believing it was wrong for anyone to own another human being. It broke my mother's heart for me to leave; she thought she might never see me again. A letter from her reached me in the month I was in Saint Louis training.

Mom wrote they were heading out west, and the land would be there for me when and if I returned. They could not stay there with me gone."

"How long have you been back, Will?"

"About three months, Thomas and me moved into the old cabin, at least what was left of it, looters had torn the place up. But we have fixed it up to be livable. And, Pastor Luke promised he would help me build a new house.

"Pastor Luke helped my Dad build the restaurant; he's a very good carpenter, Dad says the best he has ever seen."

"A week or so after Thomas and I came back, Pastor Luke showed up for a visit and asked if we would be interested in helping him build a church, mainly supplying the lumber. We said, of course. Then he invited us to Sunday morning services; said ya'll been holding service in the restaurant on Sunday mornings. Sure is nice of your folks to close down on every Sunday morning."

"Well, Pastor Luke did work for a month helping Dad to build this restaurant, they thought it only right, at least until he can build a proper church."

"Thomas and I started cutting lumber the next day after Pastor Luke visited us. We found a great stand of timber with more than enough tall, straight oaks to build the church. Pastor Luke is a very good carpenter; he learned the trade from his dad Sheriff Matthew. We grew up together in these hills, fishing up and down the river. Everyone believed he would go into the law, and he did leave Hardwood to study law, but the war broke out. Because of his education, he was made an officer. During the war, he commanded large groups of men. Many he saw go to their death, and he always said he felt responsible for their lives. He never asked his men to do something he would not do himself. He always led the charge, best man on a horse I ever saw; even as a boy, he was good bareback or saddle. So, after the war he married Fay, a girl he had met when he was in school studying law. Her family had been killed during the war. Then he decided that not the law of man, but rather the law of God is the law he needed to practice."

"Will," Elizabeth gestured toward the front door, and there came my old friend Luke with wife Fay.

I had just managed to stand, when Luke and Fay were at my side and Fay was hugging me, which always was little strange to me since she is hardly tall enough to lay a hand on my shoulder. Luke, on the other hand, just looked me in the eye; he was amazingly thin.

Odd couple to look at, but never two people man and woman better matched, surely by God himself. I do kid them about the height difference more than I should, but Luke gets me back sooner or later.

"William, we've been gone for a week; I was preaching a revival meeting over in Oakland. Lots of new families recently settled over there, and they want to start a church after the great revival we just had. We just came back into town and heard that you had been shot and that Elizabeth here had to beat a man off you. Lucky for you a man as frail as you has a woman to take up for him."

"Well, Pastor Luke, you may not have gotten the whole story, and if you keep grinning like that, I may have to wrestle you down as when we were boys."

"If you think you can, William, I am ready."

"Now, boys," Fay spoke up and then moved over next to Elizabeth and began to talk about me as if I were not in the room. "Now, I and Pastor Luke were right; he is someone you needed to meet, Elizabeth. He is not spoken for either, well not yet."

Elizabeth looked up with her brown eyes into my eyes and in a slow even tone with just a hint of a smile said, "No, not yet, is Will O'Brien spoken for."

Will clearing his throat, asked "Pastor Luke, have you seen Thomas in town?"

"Yes, I did he was down at the store gathering a few supplies. Said he figured after seeing you splitting wood the other morning and hearing the story of your tossing large men around, you were all healed up and ready to go back to cutting timber for the church. Just now, I looked up the street and I saw

Red and Blaze bringing him and the wagon this way."

"Elizabeth, come outside and let me introduce you to Red and Blaze." As I stepped off the porch; just as Red and Blaze were pulling Thomas and the wagon up to the front of the restaurant. Both horses, seeing me, nuzzled their heads to me and snorted with excitement.

"Why, William, said Elizabeth, "I believe these horses love you."

"Yes they do, and I them, but Thomas spoils them more than I do. Although he won't admit it, I have heard him talking to them as if they were people."

"Hey, Elizabeth?"

"Yes, Thomas?"

"I heard you had to beat a man off my friend William. Is that true?"

"Actually, I would rather hear about these two friends Red and Blaze. Will said ya'll brought them home from the war."

"Yes, we did; they were artillery horses used to pull a cannon and the powder and ball wagon. Every artillery horse I saw especially toward the end of the war was the most overworked and under-fed horses I ever saw. These two were no different when we found them. Gettysburg is where we got them; it was a bad day." "You do not have to talk about it if you don't want to, Thomas.

"No, that is all right, Elizabeth. I do not like talking about the war, but I do like talking about Red and Blaze. After the battle was over at Gettysburg both mine and Wills' outfits were gone, dead, or just gone, no officers to be found. Will and I spent a night around a small fire, and he told me about his home and the land. So, I had no living family to go home to, he asked me, and we started home. As we were leaving the battle field, we came upon horse artillery; all six of the horses used to pull the cannon and the powder and ball wagon were down. As we walked past them, one of the horses tried to get up, still in harness to the cannon. We both decided we should put this horse out of its pain. Standing over the horse ready to end his life, we saw the horse in harness next to him move and look at us."

"Will asked me to help and we began

to release the harness from the two horses to free them from the weight of the other four horses in the harness with them. The other four horses were clearly dead. Slowly the two horses began to come up. We stood back; a horse hurt and scared might bite or kick."

"It was a sight; the two horses seemed to be helping each other get up. They leaned against each other and pushing up little by little as they would get one hoof and then the other under and the muscles in their strong shoulders began to flex against each other. They were making noises horses make as if they were encouraging each other."

"No way were we leaving them there, not like the army needed them anymore. We found some grain in the powder and ball wagon, fed them, and led them to a stream. Along the stream, there was lots of grass, so we decided to stay and care for the horses and see if they would become strong enough for the trip back home."

"We never tied them up at night;

they stayed close, a little too close some time. Once in the middle of the night, I awoke to both horses standing their heads over me and Will. Looking out into the darkness, I could see eyes-- more than two sets, probably wolves. Red and Blaze both went a little crazy, pounding their hooves, jerking their heads up and down and back and forth. They ran toward the eyes, stopping at the edge of the woods, snorting, stooping hooves. The eyes in the dark disappeared, and both horses walked down to the stream for a drink, good friends. For me and Will they are the only good to come out that war. "

"All right William, today is Friday; we need to get to work. If you are up to it, I figure we might get back to cutting the lumber for Pastor Luke's' church."

"Gods' church, Thomas," Pastor Luke spoke up with Bible thumping excitement in his voice.

"Sorry, Pastor Luke; you are right, Gods' church."

"I am ready, Thomas. Can we stop by Sheriff Matthew's office and pick up my guns? If Thomas has my broad axe and my offset axe sharp, I should be able to finish the beams for the foundation. We can bring them with us Saturday evening, stay the night, and unload them at the site for Gods' church Sunday after services."

"William?"

"Yes, Elizabeth"

"I will have lunch for you after church."

"Thanks, Elizabeth; I will see you soon.

With Thomas at the reins, Red and Blaze took off, and I looked back to see Elizabeth waving to me. Without even thinking, I just raised my hand to her, as Thomas was mumbling, "What about me? I might want something to eat after church."

Chapter 4

"Good morning, Mister Rocman; have a seat anywhere, and I will bring your coffee."

"Thank you, Elizabeth. I will have four eggs sunnyside up, bacon, and biscuits too."

"I will put your order in to the cook and be right back with coffee."

A table in the corner next to one of the front windows allowed a man to see who was in the restaurant and watch the main street.

This little town does have potential if a businessman like me has a hand on things. If I can make a few more friends-- it does seem as if friends just appear if a person spreads a little money around... Rocman thought smugly.

"Here's your coffee, Mr. Rocman; your breakfast will be up shortly."

"Elizabeth, I heard that you folks have started a church building fund."

"Why, yes, we have Mr. Rocman not much money yet. Folks around here don't have a lot of cash to spare. Will O'Brien and Thomas Johnson are cutting the timber and hewing the lumber, and Pastor Luke and Sheriff Matthews will provide the cabinetry. We need money for nails, paint, glass panes for the windows, and a church bell to ring on Sunday mornings."

"Here, Elizabeth, put me down for one hundred dollars."

"Thank you, Mister Rocman; that is a very generous donation."

Elizabeth disappeared into the kitchen, just as Rocman was beginning to wander where his breakfast could be, Mary Lane walked out of the kitchen doors, smiling with his plate and Charles Lane right behind her. The plate placed in front of their patron, both begin shaking his hand, one then the other.

"Mister Rocman, that is a very generous donation to the church building fund," said Mary Lane. "We'll tell Pastor Luke of it as soon as we see him, and I am sure he will want to thank you personally."

"Think nothing of it, Mr. and Mrs. Lane; maybe later I can help out some more as my business grows. I look at it as an investment in the town."

"What business are you in?" asked Charles.

"Well, I buy and sell things-- land, cattle, horses, and I have just bought that large building on the south end of Main Street which I intend to turn into a house of entertainment and hotel."

"You mean a saloon?" Mary asked.

"Yes, I suppose you could call it that, Mrs. Lane."

"Seems like a poor investment; folks around here do not lean toward that kind of entertainment, drinking and such."

"Well ma'am, I'm bringing in a company of men to help me develop some land I have purchased north of town. I believe it joins land owned by the man you mentioned earlier, Miss Elizabeth, William O'Brien. The men will need a place to gather."

"Well, Mr. Rocman, we will leave you alone and let you eat your breakfast."

Eating his breakfast and looking down Main Street, he congratulated himself. This little town has no idea what is coming. Momma would be proud of my donation to the church building fund; Lord knows she never had much to be proud of, between me and Saul. Although Pa he was proud, proud of the way we could hold our liquor at an early age. He also took pride in the way we never let anyone best us. Always look out for yourself first; Pa taught us both.

O'Brien… there was a Colonel O'Brien and he was the officer who killed Pa. At the inquiry, Colonel O'Brien had stated John Rocman, while under his command, had on more than one occasion been warned about abusing civilians. On this particular occasion, Colonel O'Brien had been a witness to Pa striking a woman down at a farm house his regiment had taken. Other witnesses later stated when the Colonel had taken hold of Pa the fight was on, Pa not to be laid hold of by any man. Knowing Pa and his temper, there was no doubt there was a fight, but how did this Colonel best Pa in a hand-to-hand fight?

Pa was the best man with bare fisted fighting and mean, no rules just win and put the other man down. That's what he taught us boys. So, how did this Colonel with his bare hands best Pa? Later we heard more of the fight; that after our Pa had been beaten barehanded, he pulled a knife on the Colonel, and witnesses said they heard his wrist break when the Colonel wrenched the knife from his hand. Pa had been shot for desertion; tho' we didn't believe it was true. Colonel O'Brien, wonder if there could be a family connection between William O'Brien and this Colonel? Something we need to check into later."

"Well, to business at hand; Mary, great breakfast; may I pay?"

"Yes, Mister Rocman; that will be 4 bits."

"Thank you, Mary; I need to be

going and meet the morning stage. My hotel manager is arriving. She will be another member to our community."

"Oh, the manager is a lady Mister Rocman?"

"Yes, Mary; see you later, perhaps for supper."

At the moment Rocman stepped into the street, the stage came careening at a crazy, seemingly out of control speed, clouds of dust flying; the hollering of the driver brought the horses to an abrupt halt just feet from where he was standing. As Rocman was about to attack the driver for not having better control of his team coming into town, the door of the stage flew open, and a man tumbled out, his face-down body sprawling in the dirt. Slowly, a lady's fashionable boot moved back under a beautiful dress, and the wearer of the boot fluffed and smoothed the dress as she commented, "That should teach you that a lady goes first."

Rocman stepped over the man in the street, reaching his hand out to the lady. "Miss Cleopatra Grace I presume, you are welcome to Hardwood; may I assist you?"

"Mister Solomon Rocman why thank you. Some people do not understand the importance of treating a lady with the respect due her."

As Miss Cleopatra Grace placed her left hand in Rocmans right hand to descend from the stage, the man face down in the street was suddenly on his feet with his hand raised to strike the lady. Instinctively, Rocman elbowed him in the stomach and followed with a short, very powerful jab to his jaw. The poor fellow was back in the dirt, he was sure to be out for awhile; Rocman had used these moves a time or two.

With the support of her employer's right hand, Miss Cleopatra Grace finished her descent from the stage, planted her boot on the back of the man in the dirt, and stepped gracefully to the boardwalk.

"Mister Rocman, those two large cases on top of the stage belong to me if you can see to them."

"Yes, I will Miss Grace; driver, will you please have the lady's cases brought to the Rocman Hotel?"

"Sure thing, but where is the

Rocman Hotel?" asks the driver.

"It's the large building on the north end of town."

"Ok, but I will need some help; getting those two cases up on the stage was a two-man job; very heavy."

"Well, get some help, driver."

"I do have a helper, Mister Rocman.

"Okay, so what is the problem with the cases?"

"Well, he's face down in the dirt."

To the driver's surprise, with two quick moves Rocman reached the cases on top of the stage and sat them both on the boardwalk, saying brusquely "I will come back for one case, driver, as I need one hand to escort the lady." Addressing the lady, "Miss Grace, you only brought two cases?"

"Yes right now, your brother Saul arranged for a covered wagon to bring the rest of my things, and I believe a group of the men you asked for are escorting that wagon. They should be here in a few days."

Chapter 5

My muscles were still sore some, but it felt good to be working. Even more so since the work we were doin' was for the new church. No church ever built itself; putting up a building takes a little planning and lots of sweat. Thomas and I were good at the sweatin' part; that's why we built our sawing pit close to the spring fed creek. Work some, then go jump in the creek.

The sawing pit could sure make a man sweat, and Thomas on the other end of the two-man saw made sure I sweated plenty. Thomas may not be a big man, but I've never seen a man who could work harder or longer.

The saw belonged to Granddad; Pa and he cut the lumber for our cabin and the barn with this saw. They would both be proud to know the saw was being used to cut lumber for a church.

Now Thomas and I had decided to move the saw pit down by the creek; it had been up by the barn. There was a large flat rock jutting out from an embankment so with a platform built opposite the large rock we had our new saw pit, and it was close to the timber we were cutting.

We used Red and Blaze and some good rope to drag our logs on top of the sawing pit. Myself on the top, Thomas in the pit we began sawing logs, squaring them into beams for the rafters of the church.

By Sunday morning; foundation, flooring, partial walls, boards lay across short cut logs and a beautiful cedar Pulpit built by Pastor Luke. We were ready for Sunday morning service.

Thomas and myself came early with a load of fresh cut lumber and the beams for the roof; we had most of it unloaded when Pastor Luke showed up

We had to give him a hard time for showin' up when the work was all done. Course we knew he had been spending every daylight hour working to get the church to this point to have our first service. Even an unfinished building can house a church, he says; the church is the people, not the building. The building is great for comfort and a sense of pride.

Pastor Luke just smiled and said, "Boys, don't make me pray fire down from Heaven on you."

Well, we finished unloading the lumber and the large beams as people began to gather for the first service in the new church.

I caught a glimpse of Elizabeth; as she, along with her mom and dad went into church. She didn't go in before she threw a smile and a little, girly wave my way, makin' me grin just some. Thomas noticed, of course.

"What are you grinin' at?"

"Nothing"

"Thomas, grab hold the other end of this last beam."

I hope there will be room for me to sit by Elizabeth, I thought to myself.

We came in bout time the singin' started. Sheriff Matthew waved Thomas over to sit by him. When I saw Elizabeth, there was a place beside her. So, I went to the pew; she motioned me to sit beside her. I whispered in her ear, thanks for the seat."

She whispered in my ear, "There will always be a place beside me for you."

As the hymn Rock of Ages came to an end, Pastor Luke moved from the front pew where he had been seated beside his wife Fay and stood behind the beautiful pulpit he had built out of a cedar stump. Thomas, Pastor Luke, and I had removed it with a final pull by Red and Blaze.

The cedar tree had stood right in the middle of where we had planned the foundation of the church to be. As I began to cut the cedar, Pastor Luke asked me to cut the stump higher up from the ground than I usually would, saying he had plans for the stump.

"Friends, I stand before you this morning thanking you for the work you have already put into this church building. No walls yet, but what a great sight as we sang the Hymn *Rock of Ages Cleft for Me*, and look out into GOD'S creation."

"Turn with me in your Bibles to the book of Psalms, please. Please stand everyone stand for the reading of GODS' word. Verse 1 of Chapter one reads:

'Blessed is the man that walketh not in the counsel of the ungodly, nor standeth in the way of sinners, nor sitteth in the seat of the scornful. Verse three; and he shall be like a tree planted by the rivers of water, that bringeth forth his fruit in his season; his leaf also shall not wither; and whatsoever he doeth shall prosper.'

"I would like to speak to you this morning about this pulpit I stand behind; it was once a large cedar tree standing in the middle of what is now the foundation of our church building. Nothing worth anything in this life or the life to come is accomplished without hard work in this case by William, Thomas, and I; with the final work of pulling this stump from the ground, done by Red and Blaze. Two beautiful horses rescued from the battle field by Will and Thomas.

All around us we see Gods' hand at work. This pulpit is the beautiful finished piece that it is because of the skill and the craft taught to me by my Dad, Sheriff Matthew Jackson. Friends, only God can bless us in our work. Not so we can stand back, and say look what I did, but rather look what God helped me do. I know without his help I could do nothing………."

"The last part of this sermon is the most important; in the New Testament book of John chapter 3 Verse 16 says;

'For God so loved the world that he gave his only begotten Son that whosoever believeth in him should not perish but have everlasting life.'

"There comes a time in every man and woman's life when a decision to know God will come. That time can start with this prayer. May I ask everyone to stand and bow your heads? Say this prayer with me, if this is your time to make a decision to know GOD."

'Father in heaven thank-you for giving your son on the cross to pay for my sins. Forgive me of my sins; come into my heart and help me to know you. I ask this of you in the name of your son Jesus AMEN.'

"Friends, if you said this prayer for the first time today, I pray in the days weeks, and years to come you will begin to know GOD more and more. See you all next Sunday; God bless you everyone for coming. You are dismissed."

As I began to say the prayer with Pastor Luke, Elizabeth's hand slipped into mine. A hand soft and feminine but strong as she held my hand tightly; then her other hand reached across her body to hold onto my arm. I could hear her praying with me; then she was praying for me, praying that God would give me strength and bless everything I laid my hands to do. Not since my mother prayed for me while holding onto my hand had a lady prayed for me, and let me tell you, it felt good.

After service, we men gathered around the outside of the church to make plans for more work on the building. All the women folk had brought baskets of food, and they began to spread it out on the large beam Thomas and I had shaped for the center support for the roof. Then we rolled a few smaller logs close to the beam for seats.

Soon it was time to eat; we all gathered around, and Pastor Luke asked his dad to say a prayer over the meal.

"Son, thank you for asking me to lead in prayer. If everyone could bow our heads for prayer please. Father I thank you for this food which you have given us. Bless these hands that prepared it, and let this be the first of many meals we share with our friends and family at this Your church in the name of your son Jesus Christ. AMEN."

"Folks, let's eat," says Sheriff Jackson in a loud voice.

Now let me tell you, everyone was there, folks I had known all my life and some I had never seen.

Delicious food! Charles had smoked meat; brisket, deer hams, pork shoulder, and even a few squirrels plus two large coons.

The ladies had gone all out with side dishes from turnip greens with some of Charles' smoked bacon with just a touch of sugar to take out the bitter. Potatoes, onions, and squash pan-fried over an open pit, Charles had built just to cook at these church gatherings.

Oh, and there were pies and cobblers that for a short while when I first saw them I seriously considered eating dessert first. But Elizabeth told me it might set a bad example for the children.

After lunch some of the men from Oakland who had brought their families over for our first service were very interested in the beams Thomas and I had cut for the church since they had plans for a church.

So, I pulled out my broad axe with the offset handle, passed down to me by my granddad and I began to show some of the technique shown to me by my dad and granddad.

Much talk was given about the great revival Pastor Luke had preached for them, even talk he might have to pastor both churches. But, Pastor Luke said, "I believe God will rise up a Pastor for you folks."

After my broad axe demonstration on a log we had brought for a support beam, I began to look around for Elizabeth. Thinkin' it might be nice to walk with her down by the creek to cool down a bit.

Off aways and down by the creek, I spotted her and Thomas; as I began to walk toward them, I saw an attractive lady some years older than Elizabeth with them and by my count three children from small to medium sized.

"Hello, Will," said Elizabeth, "let me introduce you to Mistress Lillian Rose Hunt."

"Howdy, ma'am very pleased to meet you."

"And I am pleased to meet you Mr. O'Brien. I did enjoy your explaining of the broad axe carving on that beam."

"Well, Mistress Hunt, Thomas here is as good a man with a broad axe as me."

"Oh, I just believe he is!" says Mistress Hunt.

And as she was saying that, she looked up at Thomas, as she was not a woman given too much height; then she reached and touched him on the arm.

"Please call me Lillian, both of you"

"Thank you, Lillian, and my friends call me Will, except for Thomas here who has always called me William. Whose children are these?"

"They are mine. Boys, come over here; someone I want you to meet. John here is eight, Henry is five, and the girl being held by Thomas is six years old; her name is Rose. Say hello to Mr. O'Brien children."

The boys seemed a bit shy, just kicking at the ground and looking around. Rose extended her hand, her small hand seeming even smaller considering the size of my own hand inherited from my granddad.

"Mr. O'Brien," says Rose, "are you friends with Thomas?"

"I am, Miss Rose, and you may call me Will."

"Then if you are a friend of Thomas, Will, you are also my friend."

"It seems you make friends fast, Thomas.'

"Rose took to Thomas right away, Will." Lillian said. "She barely remembers her own dad who died in the war at Shiloh."

"I am sorry for loss of your husband Lillian I will say you have done well to raise these children alone."

"Thanks Will I have found work as a seamstress and I plan to open a small shop and store to sell cloths here in Hardwood."

"You know Lillian, Thomas and I could supply the lumber for your shop, after we are finish with the church building."

"Thank-you so much Will, I am going to take you up on that. Sheriff Matthew and Pastor Luke have already begun a foundation next to the Lanes' restaurant."

Lillian was talking to me but she was looking at Thomas holding her little girl Rose. Thomas, a man I had known for goin' on three years was lookin back at her in a way I never seen him look at any one before. Except maybe that Henry rifle while he is cleaning it, he does love that Henry.

"William, we need to be going, seems we have a lot more lumber to cut." Thomas kept talking to me while handing little Rose to Lillian, never taking his eyes from her face.

So we got in the wagon headed for our timber; me with the reins to Red and Blaze, Thomas looking back 'til Lillian and her children were out of sight.

Thomas was never a man to talk much; he never stopped talking about those children and Lillian all the way back to the cabin. So I say "those children need a dad" and he agreed. Then I say "that Lillian is a lovely lady and will make someone a good wife." Well, Thomas did not have anything else to say. He just went into deep thought for two days as we cut timber and lumber.

When he did talk, he asks me "what about me William?" I says "what about you?" then he asked me a question, I never thought I'd hear him voice.

"Do you think I would make a good dad to Lillian's children?"

"Yes Thomas, I believe you would. You do know that means you will need to ask Lillian to marry you."

Well his face turned red then, and for some reason he push me into the creek; may have had something to do with the grin on my face as I had to mention the marrying part.

Chapter 6

Pastor Luke had a large wagon, pulled by two of the largest mules I ever saw. Every couple of days Fay and Pastor Luke would come by and we would load up the lumber Thomas and I had cut for the church. Fay always seemed to bring plenty of lunch and then some, for us. She says most of the fixin' was done by the ladies of the church. There was this one special apple pie made just for Thomas by a Mrs. Lillian; somehow she was found out it was his favorite.

Pastor Luke and Fay even spent some time in the saw pit, with Fay in the pit pullin' on the saw. Fay is strong for a lady and not given too much height as Thomas and I enjoy commenting on, which would usually gets us the evil eye from her.

"So, I have good news, Will," said Pastor Luke "Mr. Rocman is going to chip in and pay for the glass for the windows in the church."

"Pastor Luke, is this the same man opening a saloon in town?"

"Where did you hear that, Will?"

"From Elizabeth who heard it from Mr. Rocman, and I believe there is a lady just arrived in town to manage the business."

"I will have a talk with Mr. Rocman about his business, and Fay, you may want to meet the new lady in town."

"Pastor Luke, we'll bring the last load of lumber down early tomorrow morning. While we are there, we intend on pulling some large rocks up from the creek below the church to build the front steps. Thomas wants to finish the church so we can start on another building."

"Which other building is there in town, Thomas?"

"If you must know, Pastor, we have agreed to provide lumber for Mrs. Lillian's shop."

"That is great Thomas; Dad and I

have laid a good foundation for the building."

"A fine lady she is," Fay chimed in, looking right at Thomas.

His head came up and with strong conviction in his voice he said, "Yes, I believe she is."

The moment of silence was because Thomas rarely raised his voice. We all three looked at each other grinning; the grinning turned to laughter, and then Pastor Luke lay a hand on Thomas shoulder and said, "If I can ever do anything for you, please let me know."

"Come on Fay; we best be going and leave these men to cutting timber."

Next morning Thomas and I came into town with a large load of lumber. We decided to stop and see the foundation laid for Mrs. Lillian's shop.

As we stepped down from the wagon, little Miss Rose came running and jumped into Thomas's arms clearly upset and crying. Thomas held her in front of himself so he could see her face. "What is it, child?" he asked.

"Some bad men pushed Momma down!"

"Where is she, Rose?"

"She is in our tent, lying down."

Just behind where Pastor Luke and Sheriff Matthew had built the foundation for her shop, Lillian and her children had been living in a large tent. The tent reminded me of the tents used by officers during the war down to the stove pipe access built into the roof.

Quickly Thomas, with Rose still in his arms, entered the tent to find Lillian lying on a cot clearly shook up. The two boys quickly moved between her and us, ready to protect their mother. The oldest John had a pocket knife open; the youngest Henry held a stick pointed on the end. We could see it in their eyes- nothing and no one was going to hurt their mom.

At that moment Lillian opened her eyes and saw us. Seeing her boys standing in her defense, she said, "Boys, it's ok; remember I introduced you to these men at church." Not until Thomas put Rose down, and she took him by the hand to pull him over beside Lillian's bed, did the boys back up some.

"Who were the men, Lillian?" Thomas asked

"I watched them come down the street from the saloon; the children and I were doing a little work around the foundation for the shop. They said a certain man was laying claim to the spot where I had my foundation for my shop, and I should give it up. When I told them I would not because the foundation was already down and Sheriff Jackson said the law in this town was if someone moves into town and lays a foundation for a business the land is theirs. It's the town's way of starting new businesses.

"That is completely true," I said to Lillian over Thomas's shoulder, as he now knelt beside her cot; "my granddad gave this land to the town with that bylaw attachment until the acreage given in the original deed has been used up.

Lillian said in a strained voice, "The four of them moved in close on every side of me, and one of them shoved me down. That's the last thing I remember until I awoke and saw you enter our tent."

"We carried Momma into the tent and put her on the cot" chimed in her young protective sons.

Thomas without taking his eyes off Lillian said, "William, would you go next door and ask Mrs. Lane and Elizabeth to come and see to Lillian?"

"Not at all, I will be right back."

A few quick steps and I stepped into the Lanes' restaurant; after a short explanation, the two ladies were on my heels, hurrying to Lillian's tent. I held the flap open to the tent, and as they entered, Thomas moved to let them in close to Lillian.

We both stepped outside the tent and John followed. "Thomas?"

"Yes John?"

"I got a good look at those men what hurt Momma."

"Go ahead, John; describe them to William and me."

"Well, one wore a black vest; another had brown pants stuffed inside his boots; then a darker fellow had part of his left ear gone; but the one that pushed Momma down was tall and wore a gun holster under his arm."

"Boy! You did get a good look!"

"Yea and I am takin' my knife to go find them."

Now Thomas went to his knee in front of John, looked him in the eyes, and said, "John, I think it would be best if you stayed here and looked out for your mom as you and your brother have been doin'. William and I we are going to find those men and teach them how to respect a lady like your mother."

John squared up his shoulders, held out his hand to Thomas who took it, and shook it firmly.

"My mom told me she believed you were a good man the first time she met you." He turned and went into the tent.

Thomas stood, took in a deep breath, walked to the wagon, reached for his Henry rifle, and levered a shell in the chamber. I slung my gun belt over my shoulder and put my colt navy in my belt.

The saloon had a large double door and a single side door. It was dark now, and we could see both front and side doors open; seemed like there were a lot of people in there having a good time.

Thomas stepped in the front door holding his Henry in his right hand down low. He just stood there, looking the room over. As described by John, the four men we were lookin' for were standing together at the bar.

"You, at the bar the tall feller, with the fancy shoulder holster." Thomas spoke in the loudest voice I had ever heard from him, clear intent in his tone. The room went silent with all eyes on the tall, slim man holding the large rifle low in his right hand. The man with the shoulder holster turned as did the other three.

"Are you talking to me?" the tall man at the bar said, and his hand seemed to casually reach across to the butt of his pistol in that fancy shoulder holster.

At that moment I stepped inside the side door and slammed it rather hard. All eyes turned toward me, me a grinin' and holding my rather large saddle pistol in one hand and the other hand on the pistol in my belt.

"Howdy folks, my friend here wants to have a word with some of you fellers who treated a lady friend of his poorly and with disrespect."

In that short moment Thomas had crossed the room, standing inches from the tall feller although he was not really any taller than Thomas; the Henry was now gripped in both hands. That Henry weighs a little over nine pounds with a good part of its weight in that octagon barrel. When the man turned to face Thomas; Thomas hit the man square on, holding the gun with both hands and pushing forward with such force, a crack split the air as the bones in the man's nose broke. He went down and did not move.

The man in the black vest must have fancied himself a gunman; even tho' he was looking right at me holding that Remington pistol in my hand, he went for his gun anyway.

Firing without hesitation, I saw my bullet strike him in the arm holding his pistol; he had just cleared his holster. That .44 caliber bullet made a mess of that arm; he went down.

All three of these men were standing on Thomas's left. As I fired, the man missing part of his ear just had reached out to grab Thomas. Thomas poked him in the stomach with the barrel of that Henry rifle; then as the man bent over from the blow, Thomas brought the butt of the rifle around and up which left the man lying against the bar, not moving.

The last man's hands were in the air; "Mister, I got no gun, but if you weren't holding that rifle, I'd have a go at you."

Thomas laid the Henry on the bar; as he turned, the man took a wild swing. Thomas seemed to be expecting this and had set his feet to position himself for an uppercut to the man's stomach as he dodged the man's blow to his head.

As the man doubled over and sucked in air, Thomas' left fist swung down and dropped the man face down across the legs of the man lying against the bar.

Smoke still filled the room from the firing of my Remington; I always did like the smell of black powder. Through the smoke, I could see standing in the front door Sheriff Jackson holding that double barrel shotgun of his.

As the Sheriff spoke, he casually pulled the hammers back, making a loud clicking in a quiet room and causing all eyes to focus on that short barrel shotgun. Most folks around here knew he carried that gun on his saddle while riding cavalry throughout the war. Now, as was the custom in loading a shotgun, any number of items was used for shot bits; metal, rocks, and maybe some lead. Someone holding a shotgun with both hammers back always got a lot of respect.

"Howdy, boys, seems there has been some trouble."

"Sheriff Jackson, these men came into my place of business with no reason just assaulted these four men." Mister Rocman said, as he stood and begin to ascend the stair case that went up to a balcony. The rooms opened in toward the saloon.

As I watched Rocman come down the stairs, just above him, I could see Miss Grace standing on the balcony.

"Sheriff," said Miss Grace, "I am also a witness to the brutal acts of these two men; they should be arrested and thrown in jail at once. What kind of a town is this that men can behave this way without punishment?"

"Well, it's the kind of town that does not take kindly to the mistreatment of ladies. I just left Mrs. Lillian Hunt who, by the accounting of her oldest son, was mistreated and disrespected by these four men. So, that being said and me knowing Thomas and William here; they have a total lack of tolerance when it comes to the mistreatment of lady folk, and all here should believe me when I say, these men got off lucky."

"Sheriff Jackson."

"Yes, Mister Rocman."

"The line has been drawn. You have not heard the last of this; I have friends in state government."

"Good evening, Miss Grace," said Sheriff Jackson "Thomas, William time to leave."

Chapter 7

Soon after we left the saloon, Thomas made a beeline to Lillian's tent. Mary Lane had put a bandage on her arm and one on the back of her head. She was sitting on the side of the cot, trying to convince Mary and Elizabeth she should get up and feed the children. As we men stood inside the tent and watched Mary Lane, with hands on her hips, took control of the situation.

"I'll hear none of it. Lillian, you and the children will come to our place. We will feed them and get them to bed. Thomas, help Lillian over to our place and follow me to our rooms above the restaurant."

"Yes, ma'am" Thomas handed me his Henry; then in one quick motion, reached down and gathered Lillian in his arms. As Lillian put her arms around his neck to hold on, she said,"Really, I can walk." Thomas said, "I will always be ready to carry you where ever you need to go."

Mary gave a few more instructions. "William, blow the lanterns out in the tent after Elizabeth has gathered the children some night clothes. Sheriff, don't just stand there; help me gather these children up and get them over to our place."

With the children fed and put to bed up in Elizabeth's room, Mary and Elizabeth were still fusing over Lillian, assuring her the children were alright. Thomas had carried her from the tent and upstairs to Mary Lane's own bed. He had finally left her when Mary ran him off.

As Thomas came down stairs, Sheriff Matthew had just begun to tell me what had been happening in town the last few weeks. Thomas and I had not been to town since the first church service and picnic.

Sheriff Matthew started on his second cup of coffee, all the while telling us about the last couple of weeks and the forty or so men pouring into town. "Well, let me back up cause I had to pay attention since I'm the Sheriff. These men who have come to town, mostly in wagons stopped briefly at Mr. Rocmans' saloon. Then they all seemed to be living at the old Barlow farm and lead mine. At night a lot of them came back to the saloon. By the looks of them, they are a rough lot. But, with this one exception of the mistreatment of Mrs. Hunt, they have caused no trouble."

"What do you think Mister Rocman is up to, Sheriff?" asked Charles Lane. "Lead mining maybe; but not much money in that."

"Well, I tell ya'll I did take me a look in some of them wagons that brought those men to town. There were a few tools for mining. I believe tomorrow I will take me a ride over to Oakland, and go to the land office to do a little checking. How about it, Will, want to ride over with me?"

"Sure, I'm a little curious myself."

"I'm a mite bit suspicious about how Mister Rocman purchased the Barlow place; he built that building Rocman has made his saloon."

"Wasn't it Barlows' intention to have a hotel?"

"Charles, the last time anybody saw Mr. Barlow was when he left for Memphis, to buy furniture for the hotel. Now, think about this," Sheriff Matthew continued, "two of those wagons I been lookin in, had furniture -chairs tables and such; the bar was brought in them too. Fact is, and Will you might be interested in this, Bud Tilman came in the wagon with the bar. Another man was in the wagon, at first I thought he was Rocman, but at second look wasn't dressed as nice, a little rough around the edges and some larger than Rocman, and larger than Bud for that matter."

"So, the two of them unloaded that bar by themselves and carried it in. You saw that bar, must be fifteen feet long and made of oak." said Charles.

"So we can start our investigation at the land office tomorrow over in

Oakland; are you going with me William?"

"Yes, I am Sheriff. Thomas, I suppose you will be staying here in town?"

"Yes, William, I will stay around for a few days. I am going to work on the church with Pastor Luke. When you fellers get back, we should be ready to start putting up those main beams."

"William, since you are going to the land office, can you take care of some business for me?"

"Yes, Thomas, if it's what we been talking about."

"It is, William; I have the signed paper in the wagon. I'll go get it." We exchanged a look that made everyone else in the room wonder what we were up to.

Thomas headed for the wagon; Sheriff Matthew asked, "What are you boys up to?"

"Thomas has had his eye on a hundred and sixty acre section of land for a while. It joins my family's land, and we read in a paper, if a union soldier wants to own land, he can file the paper work, take up residency for six-months, make improvements, and buy the land for $1.25 acre. Also union soldiers receive credit off the residency for time served."

"Sounds like a good start for Thomas, with him losing his family in the war. I believe Mrs. Lillian and those children sure do think a lot of him."

"Yes, they do, and you know, Sheriff, for the last three weeks since the church gathering, he has not stopped talking about them."

Thomas entered the room with his papers in a nice leather folder and handed them to me. As I took the folder, I told him, "I'll file these papers for you."

"Thanks, William, you are a good friend."

"Ok," said Sheriff Matthew. "Let's get an early start in the morning. Will, you and Thomas can sleep in the jail if you want."

"Thanks Sheriff," said Thomas, "Charles said I can stay here tonight so I think I may, and it might make the children feel safer after everything that happened this evening."

"I'm sure it would," said Sheriff

Matthew.

The back door of the jail opened into a well-kept stable. After we left everyone at the Lanes' restaurant, I bedded Red and Blazer in the Sheriff's stable and gave them some grain and a good rub down. Thomas would look after them while I was gone. Sheriff Matthew decided we would take his black and white broodmare, he always rode that appaloosa. We both decided it would be best to slip out of town before daylight and get an early start. That way we could be back in a day and a half.

I needed to stop and have a look at water-powered sawmill over at Oakland. Thomas and my saw pit could not keep up with hardwood for the building we were getting ready to start. The land offered by the town to new businesses and families moving into the area after the war, and the need for a school would catch up with our production of lumber quickly, we would need this new sawmill. Once the church is built, Elizabeth has agreed to teach younger children reading and writing.

Sheriff Matthew and I walked into

the land office, and the man behind the large counter became very nervous when we asked to see records concerning the Barlow land and holdings.

"Well", said Sheriff Mathew, "I am investigating the disappearance of a citizen in my town of Hardwood, and I wish to look at the records of his land holdings."

"Sheriff, those records are confidential, and I cannot allow you to look at them." The man really puffed himself up to attention as he spoke with chin lifted high. I noticed he was wearing what looked like a new suit and a very shiny gold chain hung from a vest pocket attached to a button, possibly having a nice pocket watch on the end of the chain. Being a land office clerk must pay very well, I thought.

"Alright", said Sheriff Matthew, "I will go see your sheriff and explain my investigation to him."

"Do what you will," said the clerk, "it will not do you any good my hands are tied; without a federal warrant or a federal auditor present, I cannot show those records."

So we turned and stepped outside, and I spied the sheriff's office up the street. "You notice, Sheriff, how his voice seemed to reach a higher pitch the more he spoke to us."

"I did notice that, William. Look, there is a group of soldiers down by the sheriffs' office."

I looked down the street toward the soldiers, a group of six standing in front of the sheriff's office holding their horses by the reins. One soldier was holding two sets of reins; the one horse was a rather large black with four stocking feet. Then I noticed another soldier, tall and large even from up the street; his uniform had the cut of an officer. His back was to me as he stepped into the sheriff's office. Something seemed familiar……

"William, let's get something to eat before we go see the sheriff besides, he seems busy with those soldiers."

"Sounds like a good idea, Sheriff, since it's close to noon."

When we had come into town, we had noticed a small restaurant; the name on the front said SPLIT PEA. We sat down and had us a good meal of brown beans and cornbread with some of the best, sweetest butter on bread I ever did eat. Sheriff Matthew may have commented on how many bowls of beans and how many pieces of cornbread I ate, I don't remember cause I was too busy eatin'.

When we came out of the restaurant, we noticed the soldiers had moved from in front of the sheriff's office to the front of the land office. So, we walked past the land office on down to the sheriff's office for a talk about the land office clerk and his total lack of cooperation.

As we walked past the six soldiers, one soldier was still holding the reins to that black horse with four stocking feet. Now we noticed these six horses and the black were well-armed. Two saddle pistols and Henry rifles on each horse; also each soldier had a side arm. As we walked by them, I nodded my head, and they all looked at me as if they knew me. I slowed a bit and looked over my shoulder at them.

"William, you comin?" says Sheriff Matthew as we stepped through the doorway "Hello, Sheriff Warren"

"How are you, Matthew? It has been a while."

"Too long; Warren, meet my friend William O'Brien."

"O'Brien you say," and he gripped my hand as he looked curiously at me. "Quiet a firm shake you got there, young feller."

"So, Warren," says Sheriff Matthew, "I'm investigating the disappearance of a Mr. Barlow over our way, and I need to see some land holding documents and the land office clerk is not being very cooperative."

"I understand your problem, Matthew; he has been cutting a wide path here lately spreading money around, says he sold some land back east. I believe if you will go see him again you might find him a little more cooperative."

"Why is that Warren?"

"The Colonel, who was just in here, is investigating some land grabbing schemes I reported. He and his men headed over there after leaving here. Come to think of it, the Colonel's name was O'Brien just like yours Mr. O'Brien. He seems like the kind of man you may

want to cooperate with starting with his
very firm hand shake.

Chapter 8

"I miss him Mother."

"Who is him, Elizabeth?"

"Why William Wade O'Brien, of course; who else do you think?"

"So that's the way it is."

"Yes, Mother, that is the way it is; I think about him all the time day and night. I think wonder if he is alright, did he get plenty to eat today, did he rest good last night. Also, I wonder does he think about me as much as I think about him."

Mary Lane reached out to her daughter laying hands on both shoulders. Pulling her a little closer, while looking into her eyes , she said,

"Elizabeth, when I was your age and I thought about a man that much, I married him, and one year later you came along; that was twenty years ago."

"Why don't you talk to Thomas, he is William's best friend. Thomas needs something to help not to worry about Lillian and those children. The children are upstairs with their mother, who is up and doin' much better. I don't think Thomas slept at all last night. He told your dad to go on to bed, and he would watch the restaurant to make sure none of those men from the saloon came by during the night. Go talk to Thomas- he is out at the table by himself workin' on a pot of coffee."

"Hey, Thomas, may I sit down? I brought out some biscuits and blackberry jelly."

"Please do, Elizabeth," said Thomas as he stood and pulled out a chair.

"You and William always stand up when a lady enters the room; thank you Thomas."

"You are welcome; Elizabeth; William and I have respect for the women folk, we were taught by our mothers and grandmothers. Then it was put into action by our dads and granddads. Just good plain manners."

Just as Thomas got a good mouthful of biscuit, Elizabeth said, "Thomas, does William ever mention me?"

"Well," Thomas said through a mouth full of biscuit and a big grin, "he said you were especially strong for a girl."

"Now, Thomas, if you can't be serious with me, I will take my biscuits and jelly back in the kitchen," said Elizabeth.

Thomas bent over the table and put his arms around the large plate of hot, fresh-baked golden brown biscuits and large jar of blackberry jelly, swallowed the mouth full of biscuit he'd been working on, looked across the table.

Without a smile and a little more seriously than Elizabeth had expected he said, "Miss Elizabeth, he has spoken of you every day since he first woke up and saw you. I have heard him speak highly of certain horses and of guns and that broad axe his granddad gave him. When William speaks of you, it is with the same care, respect, and- I may be out of place to say this but- affection, the same way as when he speaks of his mother and grandmother."

Then the grin was back on Thomas's face and he said "but he really did say you were strong for a girl." With that said Elizabeth stood quickly, threw her hand towel at Thomas, and said, "I am going up stairs to check on Lillian and the children, enjoy your biscuits, Thomas."

As Elizabeth started up the stairs, the children were coming down with Lillian behind them.

"Lillian," said Elizabeth, "should you be up?"

"I can't stay in bed forever."

"It has been only one day, Lillian," said Elizabeth. "Are you sure you feel well enough to be up and about?"

"Besides up in that room I don't hear about everything that is going on" answered Lillian.

"Ok, Lillian, come on down" said Elizabeth "you and the children can sit with Thomas, Mom will bring out breakfast. I can catch you up."

"After those men were mean to you, Thomas and William went over to the saloon with a very good description of the four of them given by John." Elizabeth's story of the accounting carried a bit of excitement, "Now the way I heard it, those men will not be able to hurt anyone for a while. The one that pushed you down is going to have trouble breathing for a while, broken nose and all. One will need a few stitches and the other two had to be carried out of the saloon."

Lillian was seated beside Thomas with Rose seated on the other side; she reached for his hand, looked him in the face, and said "Thanks, Thomas."

Little Rose lay her small hand on Thomas's. "Yea, thanks, Mr. Thomas."

"Lillian as long as I am alive no one will ever treat you like that again,' said Thomas, "but I just did what your sons John and Henry were about to go do."

"That's right, Momma; I had my knife and Henry had his stick; we were going after those men, but Thomas said it was important we stay close and protect you so we did, right Henry?"

"That's right, Momma," said Henry with his stick lying against the table beside him.

"Where is William?" asked Lillian.

"Sheriff Matthew thinks Mr. Rocman is up to something shady and he was behind those men trying to make you give up your land in town," Elizabeth explained. "They went over to Oakland. Sheriff Matthew wanted to go to the land office and check on some holdings Mr. Barlow had, and now Mr. Rocman seems to have. They should be back tomorrow."

Sheriff Matthew and I walked back into the land office and there sat the clerk in a chair against the wall; he seemed a lot smaller than before; course two of those soldier boys were standing one on either side of him. The Colonel had his back to the clerk as he was going over some folders and papers he had spread out over the large counter and a table at the back of the room. The Colonel spoke to the clerk with his back still to him and us as we entered the office. "Mister Land Office Clerk, these files are missing many documents; the ones I am the most interested in at the moment are a Mr. Barlow."

That voice! Those shoulders!

"Granddad?" The Colonel turned suddenly as I spoke.

"William!" Then he saw Sheriff Matthew; he came around the counter and grabbed us both. "How are you Matthew?"

"Just fine, Colonel" said Sheriff Matthew. "How about this grandson of yours? Looks to me he is looking you in the eye now, maybe just a bit taller even than you."

Granddad turned to face me and adjusted his gun belt some as he took a step or two around me to look me over. "You know, Matthew, I believe my grandson may have out grown me finally." Then from behind, he grabbed me in a bear hug and picked my feet up off the floor for a second, giving me a good shake and squeezing a little of the air out of my lungs. The man always was strong, next to my dad I always thought he was the strongest man I knew.

Sheriff Matthew said, "Colonel, this grandson of yours has come into his own. Back in Hardwood, William and his friend Thomas have cut enough timber and lumber to build a church. The land you set aside for a town years ago, it seems your grandson here will be the one to build the town, or at least provide the lumber for it.

"Colonel, I heard you were still in the army but what are you doing in these parts?"

"Matthew, since the war ended, many men have been going back to their homes to find the land they thought they owned taken from them. It all seems legitimate, with the documentation and all. I am working for the federal government to investigate these land grabbers. I have been given authority by the President himself to arrest and make sure the land stays in the rightful owner's hands. William, you and Matthew give me a few minutes to finish with this land office clerk, and I would like you to come to my camp south of town, and we can catch up."

The land office clerk had sort of relaxed as the attention was not on him temporarily; course that all changed as the Colonel began to speak directly to him in a tone that left no doubt here was a man that was accustomed to giving orders and having them carried out.

"Mister, I have enough discrepancies in your files here to take you over to the Sheriff and put you in his jail. Now my grandson is here, and I would like to spend some time with him and my friend Sheriff Mathew. Here is what I am going to do; are you listening? Standup, leave town now, and I will not file charges. If I hear of you in these parts again, I will make sure charges of fraud and land grabbing are filed on you."

The clerk stood slowly, looking at both well-armed and very capable looking soldiers on either side of him.

"Men," says the Colonel, both soldiers came to attention both answered "Yes Sir." The sudden movement of the two soldiers coming to attention and the quick response of the soldiers to the Colonel seemed to make the clerk ready to leave town if he had any doubts. "Escort this man out of town."

"William, I am sorry if I seemed

somewhat harsh with that man, but I have no tolerance when it comes to corrupt government officials using their office to rob honest hard working folk."

While riding out to the camp, one of Granddad's soldiers had ridden up beside me and said "When you walked by us earlier today, me and the boy just had a feelin' you must be some kin to the Colonel. Tonight is a good night to be at our campfire; the Colonel has a pot of brown beans hanging over the fire since this morning; they should be just about ready when we get into camp."

Granddad and his soldiers had made a nice camp under a large group of red oak trees on a knoll that overlooked the town of Oakland.

Well, he was right; we all ate well when we got back to camp. One of the soldiers made a fresh pot of coffee, and another soldier got busy and mixed up some cornbread batter which he put in a large Dutch oven setting in the coals of the fire. As we settled into camp, and everyone was taking care of their horses and doing a few chores, every one of the six soldiers came around and talked to me. They introduced themselves and told me how they had all been with the Colonel from the beginning of the war through to the end. The common thread among all of them was the loyalty more than just a Colonel to a soldier; it was much deeper respect that seems to me you must earn.

After the horses where cared for, we all gathered around the campfire; the soldiers all removed their hats, looked at the Colonel, and bowed their heads, as he began to pray. "Father in heaven, I thank you for the safety of my men and myself today; Lord thanks for bringing my grandson to me; bless him always. Bless also my good friend Matthew as he continues to up hold the law in Hardwood. Bless this food which you have given us and bless us as we serve you. Amen."

"Colonel, I am looking into the land holdings of a Mr. Barlow," said Sheriff Matthew.

"Now, Matthew, you know regardless of the bars on my uniform, you can call me William," said Granddad. "We have known each other since we were much younger men."

"I know," said Sheriff Matthew, "it is just that I have gotten so used to calling your grandson here William that I would rather call you Colonel, and let me say he has earned the name."

"Ok, Matthew; that would be Robert Barlow and my investigation concerning Mr. Barlow began in Memphis, Tennessee with two brothers."

Chapter 9

Milton Tipton had never received the respect he felt like he deserved, being not an especially large or strong man but doing very well in school with numbers, math, and organization. During the war, he had not fought, but because of his father's influence in the politics of Saint Louis, he had been appointed to the job of paymaster giving him the rank of sergeant. He had left the army before an investigation could be completed about moneys to dead soldiers' families.

The land office job was perfect for him, gave him the respect of town folk.

But the pay was not so good, so when Mr. Rocman came to him with a proposal that could make him wealthy, he did not think about it much.

When he entered the saloon in Hardwood, Mr. Rocman was standing at the bar. The look on Rocmans' face told whole story, he was not glad to see Tipton, and Rocman motioned for him to come into a back room.

After entering the back office, Mr. Rocman shut the door and very quickly grabs Tipton by the collar of his jacket.

"Why are you here, Milton?"

"There is a Colonel in Oakland; he just fired me from my job, and he seems to know a lot about the disappearance of a Mister Barlow. He is kin to a William O'Brien and seems to know the Sheriff of this town very well. I believe in a day or maybe two this Colonel may be here in Hardwood and I thought you would want to know, Mr. Rocman. I left town so quickly with only a horse; all of my money was in my office in the safe. I thought you could give me enough money to get on my feet?"

"You are a miserable little man." Rocman let go of him and raised a hand to strike him causing Milton Tipton to fall back into a chair.

"If you had been able to hide the documentation like I paid you to, this would not have happened, and this Colonel would not be able to touch us."

The door to the office opened and a man entered almost as large as Rocman with a striking family resemblance. "So listen, Solomon, this man wants me to pay him for his failure to do a job I have already paid him for. As if I did not have enough trouble! I was trying to win over the good folks around here, trying to become a member of the community."

"Saul, you sent your men over to try and scare that lady off her land next to the Lanes' restaurant; that did not end so well with four of our men useless for a while. Now, the local preacher man came to me today and returned the window panes I had you bring from Memphis for the new church. He said something about 'would I consider turning the saloon into some other business that did not serve alcohol?' He also gave me back a hundred dollars I had donated to the church building fund. We moved here to become legitimate businessmen. Of course, we still take what we want; but in a more quiet way, at least until we have control of enough land and money that we can make the law work for us."

"Well, Brother Solomon, Pa always said 'if you want it, take it' so far that has worked pretty well for us. The law in Memphis may not have liked our methods, it seems. Now, we have to slow down them folks building that church. When a church comes to town, the first thing to go is the saloon."

"Ok Saul, I am afraid I will have to agree," said Solomon. "Milton, I tell you what I am going to do for you; I will pay you for one more job. It will be dark in an hour or so. After dark, you go down to that new church site; there is a large wagon loaded with fresh cut lumber….steal that wagon!"

"But Mr. Rocman, I can't be caught doing something like that!"

Suddenly Solomon grabbed Milton by the lapels and yanked him to his feet, then had his feet about a foot off the floor. "Listen, little man, you will do this or when that colonel gets here, I will tell him you came to me with those land deals. I'll let him know I thought everything was legal, you being a government official and all."

"Ok, Mr. Rocman, I'll do it," said Milton. Rocman slowly released him causing him to stumble back some. "But can you pay me the money now? I will leave and go steal that wagon of lumber; I may even set fire to what they have started if it will get me some more money."

"That's not a bad idea," said Saul, "A fire would really slow them folks down building a church. Some coal oil on that foundation flooring—yeah and put some coal oil on those beams they have cut and ready to put in place.

"Milton," said Solomon, "if you can do this without any mistakes, I will pay you one thousand dollars. Take the wagon full of lumber down to the Barlow place; I have some boys there to unload it. We will use the lumber in the lead mine. If you think you can do this, there is coal oil in a shed behind the saloon;

leave now."

"Yes, Mr. Rocman, I'll go take care of this job now. That is a very generous amount of money; when will I get paid?"

"When you get to the Barlow place and I   hear the job has been done, I will send a fellow name Bud Tillman to pay you off."

Milton Tipton left the office head down like the scared rabbit he was, but both men knew he would do it and the blame would not be directly on them.

"So, Solomon that was a very generous amount you are paying that little man for such a dirty low-down deed."

"Well," said Solomon," I might have just as well said ten thousand dollars; why do you think I told him I was going to send a fellow name Bud Tillman to give him what he had coming?"

Saul gave his brother a slight grin knowing just how ruthless Bud Tillman can be. Saul almost felt sorry for Milton, but not really. Both men left the office and moved into the large room of the saloon where night had fallen and a lot of men were gathering for all nighters' of drinking and gambling. Many new men had come to town the last couple of days. Most of these men were ready to earn a dishonest buck, and the Rocman brothers would help them.

Solomon stationed himself at the end of the bar, his favorite spot to view the room. From here, he could see the entire room and have a direct view of the front door and the side door. By standing at the end of the bar, he could easily reach the short shot gun he kept behind the bar. Had he been standing there night before last, William O'Brien and Thomas Johnson could not have had such a free hand to attack those four men. He would remember and there would be a reckoning.

Solomon was suddenly aware that everyone in the room was applauding and whistling, glasses held in the air. Turning and looking up to the top of the staircase, he saw Miss Cleopatra Grace. Every evening when she came down that staircase in one of those beautiful gowns, all the men reacted this way. She was a beautiful woman. Saul had made sure the people she owed money to in Memphis would not seek her out for payment. Solomon had asked Saul, Bud Tilman, and a few of the men to be especially watchful.

Miss Grace moved down the stairs effortlessly, almost floating. It seemed every man in the room was watching her moving through the room, greeting, reaching out and touching men on their arms, having a short conversation with everyone in the room. Solomon felt a little jealous, but that was what he had hired her for, and she was good at it. She could be very friendly with a man, yet hold him at arm's length, giving just a touch on the arm and a smile making him think he was the only man for her…., it was her trade.

Miss Grace ended her walk down the stairs and across the room at the bar beside Solomon. "Who was that little man I saw leaving your office and slipping out the back door?"

"Just a business associate; I hired him to do a little job for me."

"Solomon, have you been down and seen the church the folks of this town are building? It reminds me of the church where I grew up down in Alabama, just a small town with good folks. These folks around here need that church to pull this community together. You should do something to help the town folks build that church."

"I tried to help," said Solomon, "but they threw it in my face, and you don't need to concern yourself with the community pulling itself together. I will make this community what it needs to be. The more land and businesses I own, the more control I will have. Something you might consider Miss Grace, the good folks building that church do not want to have anything to do with someone in your line of work."

"Believe me, Solomon; I know what you are saying. I have run into the holier-than-thou plenty being in my line of work as you say, but there is something different here. Did you know the Pastor of this church, Pastor Luke has a wife named Fay; she came into the saloon yesterday morning. I was drinking coffee, and she sat and had a cup with me. We had a nice chat, and she said I would always be welcome at their church. I may go this Sunday."

Solomon took hold of Miss Grace's arm and squeezed just enough to get her full attention. "If you want to keep your job and you don't want me to send you back to Memphis, you will stay away from that preacher's wife and don't concern yourself with that church."

Miss Grace pulled her arm from Solomon's grip; for the first time she was seeing a side of Solomon she did not like. He had always been the gentleman; his brother Saul was not so much the gentleman. There were rumors back in Memphis of wrong doings by both brothers; just the law never seemed to find enough evidence or someone willing to file charges. Those people always seemed to disappear. Those were the rumors she ignored because of Solomon's charm when he was with her, and she had troubles of her own which he had promised he could make go away if she moved here and ran this saloon.

"I am sorry if I seem harsh, Miss Grace," said Solomon, "but I have plans for this town and those plans do not include that church."

Miss Grace smiled at him, slowly turned and went back into the room full of men to begin doing her job. Solomon had a feeling that would not be the end of it. Never mind; she could be part of his plan or he could find someone else.

Chapter 10

I had almost forgotten how much I had enjoyed listening to my Granddad talk and tell stories; as he and Sheriff Matthew conversed back and forth about the days before the war when both of their wives had been alive. I had never really heard Sheriff Matthew talk about his wife much except for the fact she and my grandmother had grown up together and had always been good friends.

"William, your grandmother and I knew from the day you were born that God had great plans for your life. Your grandmother had a way of praying and

God revealing things to her; it was a gift she had. Your mother always amazed me at the way she could meet someone and in a short time she just had a feeling about them, sometimes good and others not so good. I believe the New Testament calls it the gift of discernment. It is a good combination between your dad and mother; you know he was always one to look for the best in people, least till they proved otherwise."

"I have not seen Mom or Dad for four years, Granddad," said William "I do miss them. There is someone back in Hardwood I sure would like Mother to meet."

"You are speaking of Charles and Mary Lane's daughter I suppose, Elizabeth."

"Yes, that is exactly whom William is speaking of, Colonel," piped up Sheriff Matthew.

"That's right, Granddad; Elizabeth did tell me about you knowing them and telling them about Hardwood, they have a nice restaurant there. Sheriff Matthew and Pastor Luke built it for them. Thomas and I cut the lumber for it."

"William, I have news of your mom and dad; they are out west in Oklahoma. I received a letter from your dad, Samuel. One of the reasons I accepted this job was I knew it would bring me to this part of the country in hopes I might be able to meet up with my family. Two things you should know, William; first is your dad and mom should be on their way back to Hardwood. It may be awhile, but that is their plans; they had no news of you, just a hope that after the war that you are alive and well."

"I have the cabin in very good shape," said William. "Thomas and I have been living there. Granddad, you said there were two things I should know?"

"So I did, William," said the Colonel; "you have a brother; he will be three years old tomorrow on September the first. I have a new grandson that I have not seen. William, your mom and dad are special people. Your mother was young about sixteen when her and your dad married; one year later you came along."

"I have missed them, Granddad,"

said William; "I know it hurt them when I decided to join the army. I did receive one letter from Mom just before I left training. She told me they were heading out West. They were to help lay out and find some good locations for outposts for the army as the country was beginning to move out West. Mom said, Granddad, recommended dad for the job with some of his contacts in the government."

"That is true William. Your dad always had a good eye for the lay of the land, and it helped that he went to school in Saint Louis to learn surveying. It was him who laid out the town of Hardwood and when he showed me his plans on paper, that is when I decided to give one acre plot of land to any new business that wanted to move to Hardwood."

"I will sure be glad to have them back," said Sheriff Matthew; "that mom of yours made the best apple pie I ever did eat. Now I'm not just speaking out of turn, but your dad is the best shot with a rifle I ever saw, what I mean is long distance. I have been hunting with him and watched him shoot the head off a squirrel so far away that I could barely see the squirrel."

"That is true," said the Colonel "from a young boy when I first started to show him how to shoot, he just had a natural ability- never had to worry about him wasting shells when he went hunting, my son was a good shot.

"Colonel, what are your plans concerning this land grabbing?" asked Sheriff Matthew. "I am going to need evidence before I can move against this Mr. Rocman who has moved into our town, and Colonel, did I tell you he has a brother, Saul Rocman?"

"Here is my plan," said the Colonel. "We are going to stay here a few more days and talk to some people who I believe this former land office agent stole land from. Some of this land was put in Solomon Rocmans name and some in Saul Rocmans. So, yes, I believe these may be the brothers I have been looking for although they don't know I am looking for them unless the land office agent went straight to them when I ran him out of town.

Maybe I should have had him put in jail. I just felt like the town needed to be rid of him. Those two Rocman brothers; there was a soldier in my outfit during the war same last name. Bad memory for me; if not for these six men, I might have killed him."

"What happened? If you don't mind to tell us about it, Colonel." asked Sheriff Matthew.

"I don't mind telling you about the man and the incident because it might let you know what kind of men we are up against. On more than two occasions, it had been reported to me that a Sergeant Rocman had gotten rough with civilians; of course, there were times we had to take supplies from farms. But I instructed my men always to be respectful of civilians and just take what we needed.

I rode up to a farm house, the forward scout soldiers' were in the front yard. Sergeant Rocman had a woman by the arm and as I observed, he slapped her across the face. I dismounted, came up behind the sergeant, laying hold of him, spun him around and caused him to release the woman. I grabbed his arm and without thinking slapped him down to the ground."

As Granddad was telling his account of what had happened, his men had all moved in close to the fire and seemed to be enthralled, listening to him tell it.

"He came up off the ground immediately and lit into me; now he was a large man and not used to being handled in that way so his blood was boiling but so was mine after seeing the way he had treated that lady. He came at me with a haymaker but missed, and I put one in his middle. It took a little of the wind out of him, but I could feel muscle hard where my fist landed. Then he grabbed hold of me; thinking I believe, to wrestle me down, but I hooked my foot behind his ankle. We both went down, me on top and weighing out about two thirty. He shoved me off him and rolled over. Then I gained my feet; he also came up quickly but with a knife. He slashed out wildly at me; then he moved in close and thrust straight in. I turned sideways to avoid the thrust, grabbed his wrist, twisted the wrist to release the knife, and heard the wrist break. Rocman went to the ground in pain.

I picked up the knife, and if these men had not gathered around me and settled me down, I would have killed him. I tell you men, it was a hard time during the war; I became a man I did not like. But myself and these six men since the war have begun a regular reading of God's word and daily praying; we are still soldiers and doing the job, but God has helped us to show mercy when it is needed."

*   *   *   *

The next morning at daylight over coffee around the fire, we said goodbye to Granddad and headed back to Hardwood.

Sheriff Matthew said, "William, I told your granddad about the church we are building; he told me when he and the soldiers get there, they will stay and help us."

"That will be good, Sheriff; those beams are going to take a lot of muscle to put in place. I can't wait to get back and start on the church."

"Is there any other reason you can't wait to get back to Hardwood?"

"Yes, there is Sheriff Matthew, I have missed her. When we are back, I am going to ask her to marry me."

Chapter 11

Sunday morning, Miss Cleopatra Grace was up much earlier than normal for her because Saturday night always ended on Sunday morning with her kind of work.

"Mr. Solomon Rocman may think he owns me. But I will go to church if I want to. I have made a living at this life of smoke-filled rooms and men who have little or no respect for women folk."

The guilt is almost unbearable sometimes; the alcohol helps, but as time goes on, it takes more and more to numb the pain, and it never really stops the feeling of guilt. All she ever wanted was to be happy; the first man promised her that he could make her happy.

Many since have made the same promise, but their selfish want and desires have always been always the same. Miss Grace had seen some men who seemed to be different. After moving to Hardwood, she saw those two men come into the saloon night before last to defend the honor and respect of one lady, neither was married to her, yet both were willing to take on everyone in the saloon to defend her. Miss Grace believes by the cut of those two; and she is a good judge of men, they would have not left a man standing if it had come to that.

Knowing the kind of woman she is the Pastor's wife, Fay Jackson came into the saloon yesterday morning to welcome me to town and to invite me to church. We sat and talk like we were best friends and already a member of her church.

So wearing a dress that did not attract the attention that most of the night dresses were designed for, she left the saloon and began to walk toward the site of the new church, all the while wondering why Solomon and Saul Rocman had made such a big deal letting everyone know they were leaving town last night but would be back Monday.

As Miss Grace came upon the site of the new church, she thought what a beautiful location. There was a foundation made from native rocks and flooring made of cut oak with four large squared posts in place. There was a rather large bluff behind the church; about two hundred yards from the building a small waterfall poured out of the rock and landed in a large rock basin that was the beginning of a small creek that ran down and around the south side of the church. Grace could see people gathering and already finding their seats; there were some ladies and one gentleman standing around a beautiful pulpit singing a familiar song known to her from days as a young girl in church with her folks.

"What a friend we have in Jesus,
All our sins and grief's to bear!

Oh, what peace we often forfeit
Oh, what needless pain we bear,
In his Arms he'll take and shield thee
Thou wilt find a solace there."

As she walked up the steps carved from large rocks then set in place and stepped onto the floor of the church; she recognized a few of the people there, those she had seen in town. A few men she had seen in the saloon, they looked at her and then quickly looked the other way. Most of them were men who work for Saul Rocman. She hoped they were not as bad as the Rocmans hoped they would be. Solomon would surely know she had been to church now, even after he had told her not to go.

Fay Jackson was one of the ladies singing at the pulpit; as soon as she saw Grace, she left her group of singers, walked straight to her and said, "Miss Grace, I am so glad you came; please come and sit with me."

Grace was still standing at the back of the church when Fay came to her. Grace said, "Thought I might just sit here on the back pew."

"Ok," said Fay, "may I sit with you?
"Yes, Mrs. Jackson,I would like that.

"Folks, before I begin my sermon, this next week when William and Sheriff Jackson get back to town, we are going to put that large beam in place and start on the walls of our church; any one with time to help is welcome. Thank you all for coming I notice we have some visitors here this morning, and you are very welcome; if you live in Hardwood, this is your church. I am glad to see Mrs. Lillian Hunt and her children here this morning all safe and sound.

"I am taking my sermon this morning from the book of Ephesians, Chapter four Verses thirty-one and thirty-two."

"Let all bitterness, and wrath, and anger, and clamour, and evil speaking, be put away from you, with all malice: and be ye kind one to another, tenderhearted, forgiving one another, even as God for Christ's sake hath forgiven you."

"Folks, the sermon this morning is

simple; we live our lives two ways. First, always in fear of want, meaning I want this and I want someone to give me something because they owe me or it is my right. This way of living is a life of unforgiveness for others and for oneself... The person living this life will take what he wants no matter who it may harm. This person cannot have friends because he trusts no one. Sounds hopeless, but it's not; life sometimes has a way of turning people away from living a life pleasing to God, but there is always hope. This life is full of bitterness, wrath, anger, loud evil speaking."

Pastor Luke raised his voice and his face turned red as he spoke the last sentence; everyone sat up, all attention on him a little startled.

Then he took a deep breath, let it out slowly, and in soft voice barley heard over the water fall behind the church said,

'Be ye kind one to another, tenderhearted, forgiving one another, even as God for Christ's sake hath forgiven you.'

This is the second way to live our lives; forgiven……..

"Here is the part of my sermon that is so simple and easy to understand. God loves you and he cares about you and he knows you personally. According to the Bible, God has known you since you were first in your mother's womb.

"Friends, here is the end of my sermon with a prayer that you may say with me, a prayer of forgiveness. Father, in heaven forgive me of my sins; help me to forgive; from this moment I give my life to you never to look back, in Jesus name. Amen."

Miss Grace looked up from the prayer she had just said; Fay Jackson standing beside her with her arm around her shoulder whispered in her ear, "I love you, Miss Grace, and God loves you."

"I feel as if a heavy load has been lifted off my shoulders," Miss Grace said to Fay.

"That is just what our Lord and Savior will do when we ask him into our hearts".

"But what will I do now?" asked

Miss Grace.

"What do you mean?" asked Fay

"I cannot go back to my life at the saloon working for Solomon Rocman."

"Miss Grace, you come home with me and Luke"

"I don't want to bring any trouble on you and Pastor Luke. The Rocman brothers feel like they own me because of some trouble they took care of back in Memphis; they will be very angry when I quit," Miss Grace barely whispered.

Pastor Luke had been standing there for enough time to hear this; everyone had left the church to go home Pastor Luke said, "We can cross that bridge when we have to; like Fay said, you may come home with us."

At the Jackson's home, Miss Grace watched as Luke and Fay prepared dinner together, their poking at each other and their way of talking to each other as if they had a secret that no one else knew. "So, this is how a man and a woman that love each other act", she thought wistfully. After talking long into the night, it was decided that Miss

Grace would stay the night and the next morning Pastor Luke and Mrs. Fay would go with her to gather her things and tell Mr. Rocman she was leaving his employment.

Sitting and eating dinner, Luke said to Miss Grace, "I believe there is trouble coming from the Rocman brothers and not just with you leaving their employment, I do not like trouble, but there are a lot of good men in this town that when it comes, we can handle this. There is a place for you in this town besides that saloon."

Chapter 12

Late Sunday night, actually it was into Monday morning, but still very dark, Sheriff Jackson and I had ridden hard to get back home so we could start on the church first thing Monday morning. Coming up the road and getting close to the creek just before we came on the site of the church, we both saw a bright light through the trees. My heart jumped in my chest, and I laid the heels to my horse, and Sheriff Jackson did the same.

Both horses crossed the creek into the church yard at a dead run; it seemed the whole world was on fire:

the church floor, the main beam that Thomas and I had worked so hard on hewing and squaring, and the two loads of lumber yet unloaded, on fire.

"William, I will go get help," said Sheriff Jackson.

That said, he laid the spurs to his appaloosa, drew his pistol, and began to fire into the air as he headed toward town. I headed for the wagons, kicked the blocks holding the wheels in place, and prayed. "Lord Jesus, help me."

With all my strength, I laid my shoulders against the wagon, sparks raining down on me; the wagon begun to move. I had already turned the tongue to point the wagon in the direction of the creek; shoving with all of my might, the wagon landed into the creek. Then I turned and ran back for the other wagon.

Looking toward town, I saw men and women running toward me; seemed like all of them had a bucket, Sheriff Jackson at the lead. As I laid hold of the second wagon, two men also began to push; one of them had a large bandage across his nose.

"Come on, boys; let's get it into the creek." With both wagons of lumber in the creek and still ablaze, men began to try and unload the lumber, but the fire was too hot.

Sheriff Jackson rode up and hollered, "William, turn over the wagons." I placed myself at the middle of the first wagon, laid my shoulders up against it, and began to push with all the strength in my legs. The wagon began to move a little; suddenly there were men from one end of the wagon to the other, and the wagon went over, spilling all of the lumber into the creek within minutes, we had also turned the other wagon over.

Now two bucket brigades had been formed. One line took buckets to put out the fire on the floor, while the other line put the fire out on the main beams. I stayed in the creek and began to fill buckets with water and hand them off as did the other men who had helped me turn over the wagons.

Looking around as I was working, I noticed those men including the man with the bandage across his nose were men I had seen only in the saloon the night me and Thomas had visited and seen some of them hanging around in front of the saloon during the day. Standing on the bank and cheering the men on and calling them each one by name, Miss Cleopatra Grace.

Some of these men- since there were enough buckets -would fill the bucket and take off at a dead run for the fire, empty the bucket, and run back for more, all the while Miss Grace calling their names, urging them on. Later, Pastor Luke told me when Sheriff Jackson came riding into town shouting 'the church is on fire' Miss Grace had run to the saloon and asked everyone in there to follow her and help put the fire out at the church. Every one of them had followed her.

As the last bucket was poured out, the sun began to come up over the bluff behind the church. Everyone was worn out; the smell of oak smoke filled the air. Pastor Luke stood in the church leaning on his pulpit; "Folks," he called out in a loud voice, "let us pray."

"Father in Heaven, thank-you for giving us the strength to put out this

fire, and thank-you O-Lord for the water from your good earth. Bless everyone here tonight that helped; give them rest as they go to their homes. Bless our hands, Lord, as we continue to build this church building for you and your people, in the precious name of Jesus Christ. Amen."

When Pastor began to pray, everyone had closed their eyes and bowed their heads; when he finished praying, the morning sun was brighter to see the damage. Pastor Luke, Thomas, and I along with Sheriff Jackson began to look at the damage.

Sheriff Jackson stood beside Pastor Luke, placed a hand on his shoulder, and said, "Son, the damage may not be as bad as it looks." That someone had used coal oil to start the fire was apparent by the smell; the cedar pulpit was wet with it but had not caught fire.

With the morning light, we could see that some of the flooring, of course, it would need to be replaced. The main beam being very green had withstood the heat. The parts of the main beam most burned, was where we would notch for the cross beams, Thomas and I had looked at it and decided it would work out fine.

The men from the saloon and Miss Grace were still working gathering the lumber from the creek and loading it back on the wagons they had by now turned back over.

"William," says Thomas, "I am going to go get Red and Blaze so they can pull those wagons back up to the church unless you want me to harness you up to them."

"I believe he could do it," said Elizabeth, standing beside William and looking at him as she said it.

Looking back at Elizabeth, William said, "Hearing you say it, I know I can."

"Hey," Thomas said with a grin, "do you two want to be alone?"

Lillian had walked up and taken Thomas by the hand; which I noticed and looking from their hand holding to Thomas, I grinned as Mrs. Lillian said, "William, who could have done this?"

Sheriff Jackson spoke up and said, "I believe the Rocman brothers are behind this, but without proof, nothing I can really do. Pastor Luke said Miss

Grace told us that Saturday night both brothers left town, and let everyone know they would not be back until sometime Monday, She said they made a big deal letting everyone know."

Suddenly we all heard a man hollering; looking toward town, we saw a man on the back of Blaze, kicking him, yanking on the reins, and whipping him with the reins forcing him to run. Red was right behind them. In a moment, they ran past us toward the creek with Red right beside Blaze; reaching out and nipping at the rider on Blaze's back.

As they reached the creek, Red got a hold of the back of the man's collar and pulled him off Blaze. Never letting go of the man, Red dragged the man up to me and Thomas and let go of him at our feet. It was the land office clerk, Milton Tipton, and he smelled of coal oil. I reached down to lift him to his feet saying, "If you hurt that horse, we will have words Mister Tipton."

"William, do you know this man?" asked Miss Grace.

"Yes ma'am; he's the land office

clerk, over in Oakland, that is until my Granddad, investigated and fired him."

"Sheriff Jackson," said Miss Grace, "I saw this man leave Mr. Rocmans' office Saturday night; when I asked Mr. Rocman who he was, he told me to mind my own business."

"Thanks. William, I believe I have more than enough evidence to arrest you, sir, and we need to find the Rocman brothers for some questions." With that I handed Mr. Tipton to Sheriff Jackson.

Chapter 13

Tuesday morning we began to work on the church after taking Monday to rest. We decided what had to be done to repair the damage done by the fire and to start back on building from there. Some of the blackened boards Pastor Luke said we would leave in place as a reminder of how God helped us put the fire out.

Middle of the morning, the Colonel and his men showed up. Now, it was a sight to see! We all stopped work as they forded the creek, the Colonel sittin' tall in the saddle leading his six able bodied and well-armed men.

The Colonel dismounted as he gave the command to dismount to his men; then he walked straight to Pastor Luke, shook his hand, and said, "Pastor Luke, I am sorry about the fire. We met a man up the road a ways and he told us all about it. Just looking back now I believe I should have had the land office clerk put in jail; my men and I are here to help until the church is finished."

"Colonel, I am sure you did what you believed was fair to Mister Tipton at the time; how could you have possibly known he was would head over this way? Not your fault, Colonel O'Brien; besides now that you are here, maybe I can get some work out of that grandson of yours."

"Where is he?" asked the Colonel.

Thomas walked up about that time. "Colonel, William and Elizabeth took a break and walked over to the water fall." Thomas stood very straight as he spoke to the Colonel.

"You must be Thomas," said the Colonel, as he stuck out his hand. "William has spoken of you, and Sheriff Jackson tells me you saved my grandson's life. Son, I am very glad to meet you, very glad."

"I was just returning the favor," said Thomas; "on more than one occasion William save my life during the war. Colonel, would you like to look at some of William's work?"

"Are you talking about that large main beam and those support beams? William from the time he was strong enough to swing a board axe caught on quickly, and had a better eye than his dad or myself when it came to squaring a beam. Looks like you boys have notched the beam, and it is ready to be put in place."

"Yes, it is," said Thomas. "William said when you and your men got here, with ya'lls' help; we could put the main beam in place along with the support beams. We have some good ropes and pulleys; just need the muscle and William to get back with Elizabeth."

"That looks like soldiers just rode up to the church," said Elizabeth, "and I am sure the big man in the lead is your granddad. I have not seen him since I was a little girl, and he first told me about you."

"That's him," said William, "We need to get back over there; with them arriving, we'll have the main beam and support beam into place much faster. Say, Elizabeth?"

"Yes William."

"After supper tonight, I would like to ask your dad if I can marry you."

"Maybe you should ask me first, William."

"I thought I just did," said William with a puzzled look on his face.

"No" said Elizabeth, "you said you wanted to ask my dad if you could marry me."

Elizabeth took a step back from William and folded her arms; well, if he wants me to marry him, he has to ask me, she thought to herself, but if he don't hurry and ask, I may say yes before he asks.

William reached out and took Elizabeth gently by the shoulders, looked square into those brown eyes and said,

"Elizabeth Lane, will you marry me forever?"

"Yes!" So quickly did she answer

that he wondered why she had made such a big deal about him not asking her directly. Of course, if he were going to ask her dad that meant he wanted to marry her but since she had grabbed him around the neck and was holding him tightly, he guessed he had asked her properly now.

Looking up with Elizabeth's arms still wrapped around his neck, he saw the Colonel and Thomas walking toward them.

As they got close, the Colonel said, "Young lady is it proper for a young unmarried lady to be holding on to my grandson in that manner?"

Elizabeth released her hold on him, turned to the Colonel and said, "It is if she is to be his wife."

"Congratulations, William." said the colonel. "This little girl I first met in Gettysburg has grown to be quite the lady. I needed a granddaughter." The Colonel said this with just a little crack to his voice; he shook my hand and Elizabeth hugged him.

Thomas slapped me on the back and said, "William, what took you so long to ask her?"

"Well," said William, "there was a fire and those men I had to help you with and Sheriff needed me to go to Oakland with him."

"Looks like our friend Pastor Luke will be busy; last night with the permission of her children, I asked Lillian to marry me and she said yes," said Thomas

"Well, now men," said Colonel O'Brien, "how about we go finish building this church so these ladies can have a proper church wedding?"

With the help of the Colonel and his soldiers we soon had that main beam and the support beams in place. Now, time for the roof and the walls; the roof would be made of cedar shingles, cut from the same cedar tree Pastor Luke had built his pulpit from. Other large cedar trees had been cut to make pews and two altars.

With the beams in place, Pastor Luke and Sheriff Jackson began to frame in the walls; the soldiers went to work cutting the cedar logs in lengths for the shingles. We ended up with four froes and wooden mallets to split the cedar blocks into shingle and shakes for siding.

After supper that night, I was nervous about asking Charles Lane if I could marry Elizabeth. I think he knew the question before I asked it; I know Mary Lane knew. I was sure Elizabeth had told her right away by the way Mrs. Lane kept hugging me during supper at the restaurant. Boy, did she ever put a lot of food on my plate which I was obliged to eat.

Charles gave us his blessing; I had asked him to step outside before talking with him. Afterwards, he came back into the restaurant announcing our betrothal to everyone, which caused Elizabeth and I to blush just a little.

*   *   *   *

We noticed there was not a light in the saloon, and no one had heard or seen the Rocman brothers. The Colonel and his soldiers had made camp down by the church. Also many of the men that were in Rocmans' employment that had helped us put out the fire decided to build a camp down by the church. The fellow with the broken nose had spoken to Thomas and Pastor Luke saying his momma had raised him in church, but during the war he had fallen in with the wrong crowd so he and the rest of the men from the saloon would make sure no more damage was done to the church. They would stay in town to help finish it. Also, with hat in hand and Thomas present, he had spoken to Mrs. Lillian Hunt asking her to forgive him of his ill treatment of her. Being the lady she is, she had told him she forgave him and offered her hand.

While all the women folk had gathered up at one table in the restaurant to make wedding plans for me and Thomas, we decided it would be a good time for us men to go to the Colonel's camp and make plans for the work day tomorrow.

*   *   *   *

Pastor Luke, Thomas, Sheriff Jackson, and I walked upon the soldier's camp to find my granddad standing up in the light of the fire with the six soldiers and all of the men from the saloon listening to him reading from the Bible in a voice that took me back to when I was a small boy. I heard again Psalms 23:

'The Lord is my shepherd; I shall not want. He maketh me to lie down in green pastures: he leadeth me besides the still waters. He restoreth my soul: he leadeth me in the paths of righteousness for his name's sake. Yea, though I walk through the valley of the shadow of death, I will fear no evil: for thou art with me; thy rod and thy staff they comfort me. Thou preparest a table before me in the presence of mine enemies: thou anointest my head with oil; my cup runneth over. Surely goodness and mercy shall follow me all the days of my life: and I will dwell in the house of the Lord forever.'

Granddad closed his Bible, held it in his left hand over his heart, and said, "Men, this book given to us by God, tells you that God knows you and he cares what happens to you. He prepares a path for us to follow and if we trust in Him a life can be lived with honor and respect. No matter your past, if you ask God to forgive you, He will and from tonight on you can be back on the path He has prepared for you. Men, let's pray and in praying, pray for our work tomorrow on this church we build for the glory of God."

The sounds of men praying around a camp fire was a sound Thomas and I had heard many times during the war, but this praying was different. Those men had been praying out of fear of dying tomorrow. Tonight these men were praying to a God that had forgiven them of their sins, and they were praising him for that mercy.

*   *   *   *

After Granddad's Bible reading and prayer, it was decided that Thomas and I would go get another load of lumber we had cut for the church while everyone else was splitting cedar shakes and shingles, and they would begin building the roof and roughing in the walls and windows.

As it was just starting to become light, we began hitching Red and Blaze to the wagon. We both took a look at Blaze's mouth, as it was still a little sore from the roughness of Mister Tipton; he had been yanking on the bridle forcing Blaze to obey him during his failed escape. Those two horses were sure glad to see us.

I told Thomas even with the trouble at the land office in Oakland I had made sure his land claim was filed properly. If we could build a water-powered saw mill, building lumber would come much faster and easier, and we could retire that two man hand saw and the pit. We both agreed that would be good.

By noon we had loaded the rest of the lumber we had cut and the two-man saw we had thought we might need to cut some lumber on site.

I decided to walk up the hill to Grandmother's grave, and Thomas said he would go down to the creek where he had left Red and Blaze. By the time he rounded them up and got them hitched to the wagon, I should be back and ready to go.

Grandma Mary's grave on top of this hill under this large red oak had always been a favorite place of mine since she had passed.

I sat there thinking how much she would have loved Elizabeth; I knew Mom and Dad were going to love her also. I have a little brother? I can't wait to see them. I do wish Grandma Mary could see this church when it is finished; she will I am sure, looking down from Heaven.

Walking back down the hill toward the wagon wrapped up in my thoughts of Grandma Mary and Elizabeth, I noticed Red and Blaze hitched to the wagon, but Thomas was not alone. Holding a gun on Thomas was Bud Tilman; standing just to Thomas's right was Solomon Rocman. Out of the right corner of my eye I caught movement; I turned to see Saul Rocman step out from behind a tree holding a rifle on me.

"Well, now, Mr. O'Brien," said Solomon Rocman, "how 'bout you just come a few steps closer and drop that gun belt; you seemed mighty handy with that Remington back at the saloon." Pulling back his jacket, he said, "As you can see, I don't carry a weapon; I prefer to take care of men who cause me trouble with my hands."

"I heard you also take care of women folk who causes you trouble with your hands; that must make your momma proud and make you feel the big strong man pickin' on women, or so I heard from a lady name Miss Cleopatra Grace."

I thought they had the advantage now but if what I believed is true about Solomon Rocman, he is going to want to fight me hand to hand, so why not make him mad; might give me a little edge. I could tell by the expression on Solomon's face and the sudden removal of his jacket it bothered him.

Solomon spoke with a tone in his voice of contempt and hate. "Saul just wanted to shoot you; I want to kill you with my hands. We have learned that a certain Colonel O'Brien was responsible for the death of our father. So our revenge will be on you since this Colonel has also ruined our land grabbing scheme. So Saul and I decided to compromise; he gets to shoot you, but not kill you, shoulder maybe, leg maybe, and then I will finish you off. If you really are as strong as everyone says, it should still be a good fight. Oh, and Bud here is going to shoot your friend Thomas."

I heard Saul move up behind me, and I heard the hammer on his rifle cock. Across Solomon's left shoulder and up on the bluff that overlooked our land, I thought I saw a movement; then there was a puff of smoke, a bullet whipped past my ear, and a delayed crack of Sharps .52 caliber sounded followed by a noise as if someone had fallen to the ground behind me. I turned and saw Saul on the ground a patch of blood on his right shoulder; he was not moving. I turned back around to face Solomon; he was coming at me fast. Then I saw another puff of smoke from the bluff, heard the delayed sound, and the rifle breach in Bud's hand exploded, him letting out a yell.

Solomon was on me, but before he had gotten to me, I had set my feet. His first blow swung wild with rage, I dodge it with a turn of my head and a slight arching of my back. Catching his arm as he swung, I spun him around and slapped him hard with an open hand calloused by years of hard work.

This, of course, fueled the anger and rage in the man as I knew it would. This time he came in slower; I could tell by the way he was moving and trying to set me up, he had some training in bare knuckles fighting. Solomon was a big man, tall as me and quick; I give him that. I landed a good solid punch to his midsection, and there was hard muscle there.

He begin to land punches to get in close; then he pushed me away and started coming in again, setting me up for each blow which hurt but we both knew these blows from either of us would not take the other one out, so the grappling began. He reaches in and suddenly had me on the ground; he was quick. In a moment he had a knee in my chest and had drawn back a fist aimed at my head. Grabbing the knee on my chest, I shoved with all my strength; Solomon went rolling.

At that moment, I knew I was the stronger man; he knew it too. As he began to get up, he pulled a rather large knife from his boot. We began to circle, him slashing out with the knife and me dodging. Thomas hollered to get my attention as he threw me a rough cut four by four; as I caught it, Solomon came in fast and high with the knife slashing downward.

I raised the board to block the knife; it stuck solid in the board. He was gripping the handle of the knife trying to free it from the board when I twisted hard catching him hard on the side of the head. Solomon went down quickly and hard, not moving. I just stood there letting one end of the board drop to the ground the knife still in it; exhausted I looked down and saw blood on both ends of the board; I looked up at Thomas. He said "I hit Bud with it, and there lay Bud out cold."

We heard horses coming fast from the direction of town; it was Sheriff Jackson and Granddad with his soldiers. Riding up and dismounting, Granddad said one of the men from the saloon that had been in his camp last night fesses up this morning. Said he knew the Rocman brothers were watching and waiting for William to leave town planning to kill him.

Saul was not dead; the soldiers patched up his wound. Solomon and Bud came around slowly; we found their horses, put them on them, and the soldiers put them in hand cuffs. Sheriff Jackson said they would stay nice and comfy in jail with Mr. Tipton.

The Colonel explained to the Rocman brothers that with the evidence he had on them, he would be taking them back to stand trial in Memphis.

Sheriff Jackson was curious as to how I managed to shoot Saul and shoot the rifle out of the hands of Bud.

"There was a rifle on that bluff over there; both shots sounded like a Sharps to me."

"Only one man I know could make those shots, your dad, Samuel O'Brien. That road on the bluff comes through town before getting up here. I say your mother and dad will be waiting for us in town.

"Don't forget the little brother," I said.

They were in town, Mother ran towards me as soon as she saw me coming; I jumped from the wagon to meet her and hug her. We walked arm in arm toward Dad standing there in front of the church holding that Sharps rifle a small boy holding on to his britches leg.

"Hey, son, how are you? Meet your brother James O'Brien."

Epilogue

It has been two weeks since the Rocman brothers showed their hand. Pastor Luke has visited them every day in jail; he said God cares about all men no matter what wrong they have done. Granddad the Colonel has kept a soldier posted at the jail to help Sheriff Jackson and two men at night.

Sunday morning service, main beams are in place but we are still working on roof and siding. The rest of the men the Rocman brothers had hired were in church. Some of the men that had received Christ at Granddad's campfire went out to the Barlow mine and invited them to church; Sheriff Jackson went with them and told them there were no charges against them if they didn't cause any trouble.

At the end of service, Pastor Luke invited anyone who would like to know Jesus Christ as their personal Savior to raise their hand; all of those men raised their hands and then said a prayer of salvation with the whole congregation.

As soon as service was over and before lunch, Thomas and Lillian were married. I was very proud to stand with him as best man and Lillian had asked Elizabeth to be her maid of honor.

Standing there looking across at her, I was thinking next week it will be us gittin' married, and if it had been up to me, we would have gotten married the day I asked her. Mary her momma had said I could wait till the church was finished; besides apparently Mary and Lillian were building her a wedding dress.

One of the soldiers played a beautiful melody as Lillian came down the aisle. Her two boys John and Henry both were giving her their arms and Rose was leading the way, slowly dropping flowers along the way, flowers she had picked herself.

During the ceremony, Pastor Luke told how great it was that God had brought these two people together, a husband for Lillian and a father for her children, a wife and family for Thomas.

After the wedding the man with the broken nose and the other three men who had mistreated Lillian came to her and Thomas hat in their hands and all four wished them the best in their future.

It was known by some that earlier in the week while they had been working on the church that Lillian had noticed their clothes were in bad need of repair. She had offered to do some mending for them and they accepted. When she was all done, they had offered to pay her, but she had told them no charge. So, they had sneaked around and given the money to Little Rose. I believe those men would take a bullet for Lillian.

*   *   *   *

The following week the church building came together very quickly with so much help. We had no window panes so Pastor Luke built window shutters that could be opened with a rope and pulley system; behind the pulpit there were large windows to open and give a view of the water fall during special services like a wedding.

The Colonel had a conversation with Miss Cleopatra Grace and told her that he had contact with Mr. Barlow's son; he was willing to have her start a business in the saloon if it were not a saloon but a hotel as his dad had originally built it to be. They talked much of the trouble she had had in Memphis. He said he would look into it, and she might have to appear in court to straighten some of it out, but with his recommendations and the folks of Hardwood, the Colonel told her things should work out. Miss Grace told the Colonel he and his men would always have a room in her hotel if they needed it.

Finally, my much anticipated day arrived. "Folks, we are gathered here today in the sight of God and those present to join these two William Wade O'Brien and Elizabeth Faith Lane in holy matrimony. God gave us the best of examples how two people should love and live their lives together. He first loved us so much that he gave His only Son for our sins to be forgiven. A marriage has to be totally selfless thinking only of the others needs.

"William, Elizabeth, First Corinthians 13:13 says,

'and now abideth faith, hope, charity, these three; but the greatest of these is charity.'

"If you will both always have faith in each other, if you will always have hope for the future, if you will always be charitable toward each other, God will take care of the rest."

*　　*　　*　　*

As I sank the double blade ax deep into the trunk of the tree, it came closer to coming down, Elizabeth's new house needed furniture, and there was a baby bed to build.

A man's work makes him strong.

The love of a good woman makes him stronger.

Lightning Source UK Ltd.
Milton Keynes UK
UKOW04f0335151214

243121UK00001B/1/P